KING
OF THE
BASTARDS

WWW.APEXBOOKCOMPANY.COM

KING
OF THE
BASTARDS

STEPHEN SHREWSBURY
BRIAN KEENE

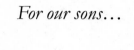

For our sons…

ACKNOWLEDGEMENTS

Both authors would like to thank Jason Sizemore, Lesley Conner, Maggie Slater, Justin Stewart, Daniel Kamarudin, Paul Goblirsch, Leigh Haig, John Foley, Kyle Lybeck, M. Wayne Miller, Mark Sylva, Tod Clark, and Stephen McDornell.

Steven Shrewsbury would like to thank Stephen Zimmer, John August Shrewsbury, and Aaron Shrewsbury.

Brian Keene would like to thank Mary SanGiovanni and his sons.

THE SAGA OF ROGAN,
OR
WHAT HAS GONE BEFORE

From the Book of the Yidde-oni

ROGAN WAS BORN in a savage age before the great flood. Cut from his mother's belly by his father, Jarek, during a raid in Larak, Rogan was raised into barbarism among the fabled Keltos folk in the Caucaus Mountains, where violence was a way of life.

Roaming the lands north of the Black Sea, Rogan grew strong and hard amongst his rugged kin. But he wearied of a life disrupting the obsidian trade from the East, and raiding the great cities of Chanoch, Urak, and Jericho. So Rogan journeyed west, crossing the land bridge at Bosporus. The accounts of his adventures during this time have been lost in the deluge.

Eventually, he became a mercenary for King Akhensobek, ruler of ancient Kemet. Rogan lead the king's armies, until a tryst with the royal daughter aroused Akhensobek's ire. As punishment, Rogan was walled up alive inside the great idol of the reclining cat god, Bastet. After a miraculous escape, Rogan slew the King and returned to the primal kingdoms of the north.

Cutting a bloody swath through the lesser realms of Lascaux, Agudea, and Gordes, Rogan became a leader in the revolutionary forces of General Thyssen. The two men became great friends and comrades at arms. Thyssen wished to oust Silex, the cruel ruler of the grand realm of Albion. The revolution ended when Rogan seized the crown from Silex's decapitated head and placed it on his own.

Rogan's rule of Albion was stern but fair. Thyssen was given command of Albion's military might. Border clashes with savage Prytens and their savage Queen Tancorix kept them busy for decades. Rogan wed Thyssen's sister, Desna, and sired an heir, Rohain. Several more children followed and Rogan came to know contentment, however fleetingly. After the death of Queen Desna, however, Rogan grew weary of palace life and abdicated his throne to Rohain.

Accompanied by his nephew Javan, the youngest son of General Thyssen, and his two Alatervaeian bodyguards, Rogan journeyed across the western ocean, discovering fabled lands and new cultures far to the south in the new world, beyond the edges of scholar's maps. There, Rogan set about adventuring again with the aide of new friends from the mysterious realm of Olmek-Tikal.

But, as our story continues, Rogan soon learns that no matter how far one travels, the past can still reach out to haunt the present...

"Living, I was your plague— dying, I shall be your death."

Martin Luther

"What you really wanted, you could never have. You needed a tragic father to give your life meaning."

Tom Piccirilli – *November Mourns*

PROLOGUE PRELUDE TO A YARN

"COME, YOUNG ONES. You grow weary of our journey across this endless sea? Sit down and I will tell you a tale of your grandfather."

Sweeping back his long black hair, the tallest youth looked at his father and then at the waves beyond the edge of their craft. "You mean Grampa, who tends the animals down in the hold and cleans the shit from their stalls?"

"No, not him, Gomer! While a fine man, your grandfather down below was not an adventurer. I speak of your *other* grandfather, the man from whose seed your mother sprang."

A second boy settled in on the deck. Unlike Gomer, his hair was blonde. Despite the contrast, they were clearly brothers.

"Is it true he was a savage warrior?"

"Yes, Magog, that is so. Your grandfather was a man of great power. He made himself into one of the most feared men of the olden realm. He was a fighter and a king, a man who laughed at the birthplace of thunder and lightning."

Gomer did not look up from the rolling sea. "Was grandfather king of the entire old world?"

"No, he ruled but a small part of it. But he was known, feared, and lusted after throughout the entire old world. Kings, women, brigands, and bards—all knew his name. It is whispered that he was known even in the depths of Hell itself. Indeed, some say he was known throughout the Labyrinth."

Many of the children blinked at this assertion, but Gomer continued to watch the sea. Below their feet, deep within the bowels of the ship, a horse neighed. The sky seemed to grow darker.

"It is too bad he isn't here with us," Magog lamented. He followed his brother's gaze, eyeing the waters surrounding the boat, hoping that the others would not notice he was trembling. He feared the huge reptilian shapes that reared up, watching them from afar with cold, obsidian eyes, before vanishing into the depths again.

"It was not his destiny to live on this way," their father continued. "But listen now, and I will tell you of a tale late in his life, when he too was on a long journey over the sea. Perhaps his courage will take your mind from our plight. He too was nearing unexplored lands and mysterious places— far, far beyond the edges of the maps of that time. He faced an uncertain future, just as we do."

The boys' expressions grew troubled.

"Look out at those waves," their father said. "Your grandfather sailed and fought over this very same sea. Beneath us, the Earth twists on its foundation, re-shaping, changing its face. In your grandfather's day, it was not such a cataclysmic time. Yet even then, things were never simple.

"Come, my sons, and I will tell you the beginning of the tale of the bastards of King Rogan!"

1 ON THE HORIZON

THERE'S BLOOD ON *my hands and something is coming for me...*

Rogan, the former King of Albion, was used to both.

Having his hands sticky and slick with blood had never stopped him from either holding a baby or taking a life. More blood ran down his palms now as he squeezed his hands tighter. Memories, ghosts, and a nagging sense of dread filled his skull. His fingers—fingers that had put out eyes, ripped open jowls, and cleared the snot from children's faces—burned. The sight of his own blood reminded him of something deep, coarse, and primal in his nature. Be it from the Magus whose head he caved in at age eleven (while using the stone penis of the god Marduk as a club) or the King of Kemet who he slew ten years later (after he hung Akhensobek's one hundred and fifty children on the Avenue of Obelisks), Rogan was used to bleeding himself to accomplish a goal.

As he did now.

The sensation of being pursued by something dire wasn't an alien emotion either. Just not one he'd recently experienced. Rogan wrote it off to his own madness from the wine and pickled beef of the sailors he currently abided with, and focused on the task at hand.

Or rather, the task at bleeding hand.

"Fight him, my Lord," a sturdy youth exhorted. "His life is yours to claim!"

Feet planted on the lip of the tubular, wooden bireme vessel, Rogan yanked back on the fishing rod. The boat rolled beneath him. Bare-chested sailors cheered his actions.

"By Wodan," Rogan swore, "this fish fights like a Stygian whore, Javan." Ruddy calluses twisted the pole and Rogan's rage increased. His thick limbs still surged with power, even though he had just passed his sixtieth summer. Muscles strained the ragged edges of his sleeveless deerskin tunic. Gnarled fingers worked deftly, age not slowing their speed or prowess.

"Lay on," the sailors on the craft shouted in hearty support. "Fight him, Rogan!" A few of them elbowed each other in their exuberance, leading to shoving and brawling as the big man battled the fish.

The scars of battle lined the former monarch's sunscorched face. A shadow of hard living permanently creased his forehead and even more lines now appeared around his gray beard as Rogan fought.

"Damn," he grunted. His somber brow furrowed beneath windswept locks of silver hair. A few strains of auburn still swam in his scalp. He braced his heavy boots against the bireme's retaining wall, leg muscles bulging in his trousers. A few of the slaves rowing the vessel looked at him and then smiled at each other, shaking their heads. He glared at them. For a moment, he considered abandoning the fish and breaking their necks instead.

Done with their squabbles, the lean, ginger-skinned sailors from Olmek-Tikal turned back to Rogan and smiled, enjoying the mighty foreigner's exhibition. They shouted wagers to one another, gambling on everything from the size of the fish to how long it would take Rogan to land it. Descended from the last remnants of sunken Atlantis, they gladly served Rogan, rewarded with adventure, women, and the promise of gold, hidden in the depths of their own shadowy continent. Their garments were frayed from exposure to the elements, sustained during this long trip of coastline fishing.

Rogan's bodyguards looked on as well. Both originally hailed from the icy lands of Alatervae north of Albion. The immense, blonde warriors sported bushy beards over squared, granite jaws. Their sinewy bodies, stout as tree trunks, easily carried the heavy steel slung from their thick belts.

One of them elbowed Javan. "Lots of fight in the old man yet, aye?"

Javan winked at the Alatervaeian, then gave him a stern look as if to dissuade him from further comments. He spoke loud enough for Rogan to hear him over the cheers of all aboard.

"Heed thy words, Wagnar. You and your brother Harkon may indeed wear the regalia of the Royal Blue Aitvaras Guards, but make no mistake. You will regret jeering the king."

Turning, Rogan's icy blue eyes pierced the guard. He cursed the man in his native Keltos tongue, not caring that the guard couldn't understand him.

Wagnar grinned, oblivious to the curse. Rogan switched to Albionese.

"I'll have your sack for that, Wagnar," he growled. "This fish will break before I will. No spawn of the sea will best me."

The bodyguard's face turned red, either from suppression of laughter, or wonder at the threats of the old man.

Smiling thinly, Rogan turned to Javan. "Ready an arrow, boy. Your father, General Thyssen, taught you to shoot. It's time again to display those skills."

All eyes were fixed on Rogan, even the slaves, chained to the oars, seemed engrossed in the display. Rogan worked the reel, a primitive pulley system where he wound back the thin cord. More of his blood dripped from his fingertips, splattering onto the deck. He took a deep breath, held it, and pulled. A great fish jumped from the ocean. It was bottle-nosed, with an immense, reptilian fin on its back and rows of flashing scales.

Javan gasped. "I've not seen anything like it!"

"Tis a denizen of Dagon's realm," Wagnar breathed. "This is a bad omen."

His brother, Harkon, nodded in agreement, mouthing silent prayers, drawing the *T* sign over their hearts in reverence to their god, Thunderer Donar Tanaris.

In his declining years, Rogan's body had lost plenty of mass, but none of its strength. Over the next hour, his savage determination never wavered as he fought to land the fish. Eventually, with the aid of three well-placed arrows from Javan's bow, it laid thrashing on the deck of the vessel.

"There's your goddamned omen," Rogan taunted his guards. "Just a fuckin' fish, that's all. No spawn of Dagon." He took a deep breath. "Omens are excuses the priests use to scare people. Still, I'll admit that they do have unusual animals in this land."

Rogan waved a weary arm toward the horizon. He almost expected to see the northern lip of Olmek-Tikal, but instead there were only a few large birds in the clear, blue sky.

Javan nodded, eyeing the birds. "Strange things live near the unknown continent, Rogan. We are close to the coastline this day and yet far from these sailors' homes in the lower Isles. According to Captain Huxira, we are nearing the waters of a tribe called the Wando-Tallan. Most nights we have put down on an island, but this night I fear we will go to the mainland."

"Fear?" Chuckling, Rogan rubbed his left bicep, watching the score of men row the long craft. "I saw but the edge of this here land and its islands before. The insect infested glades and swamps of that realm are not for me. That's why on this journey we have ventured farther north—away from such swampy mire."

Javan scratched his forearms in memory of the insect attack.

Rogan continued. "Farther inland on this vast continent, there are mist-covered mountains and a lost city with streets paved of gold."

"So they say," Javan muttered dryly.

"Our companions whisper of a race known as the Anastazi, as well as a great serpentine mound, a gigantic waterfall to the north, and a canyon in the far west that reaches into the very bowels of the earth. I would see these sights and the other wonders of Olmek-Tikal before I breathe my last."

"And I shall see them with you," Javan agreed, cracking his knuckles. "As my father did before me."

"Your father is a good man for an old prick. I see his strength in you, Javan." Rogan rubbed his hands together and stared at a scar on the back of his left hand. In a quiet voice, he asked, "Tell me, do you think of him often?"

"After battle I do, or when we encounter something like this." Javan prodded the fish with his foot. "I am no bard or poet, Rogan. When I sit again in my father's house, I regret that I will lack the words to tell him of the things we've seen."

"Aye," Rogan nodded, his thoughts turning to his son, Rohain, who now sat in Rogan's abdicated throne. "But your words are far prettier than mine."

While the sailors gutted the fish, Rogan strode to the edge of the ship. His movements still fluid even if he moved slower than in years past. His joints echoed the battle with the fish, but he didn't let it show.

Javan looked again at the waves around the ship, took note of the rougher waters and said, "So there will be new adventures here, sire? A tour, perhaps? I know a hunt will be mandatory once we make landfall, at the very least, if only to escape the tedium of life on this vessel."

Rogan laughed, reading his nephew's mind. "Between you, me, and the sea, Javan, my mouth may have overloaded my arms."

Javan spoke silently so the others did not hear. "Sire?"

"I found palace life a bore," Rogan confessed. "That's why I gave the crown to Rohain and left Albion. My son is better for that life than I am, even if the same storm flows in his veins. He has some of his mother—your father's sister—in his veins to add balance."

"I know, sire. It was his time and thus, your soul drifted elsewhere." Javan's eyes were drawn to the sky, and the enormous birds circling there. One was much larger than the rest. "But many wonder if my cousin will live up to your rule."

"Rohain will make them eat those damned words. I cannot find favor with all by abdicating a throne I fought so hard for, but I couldn't sit in my bed any longer. When I went back to Albion, I heard the whispers and gossip. That was when I took you with me. I have not been back since. My only regret is that perhaps we should have also brought along my other son, Teran."

"I thank you for your favor in this adventure, sire."

Again, Rogan waved as if the continent would appear any moment. "Returning for a tour of North Olmek-Tikal in search of adventure is mayhap a silly thing. I know what others say of me. 'Old man trying to find his young self.' Bah. Wodan take them all to Hell. When I bedded the Pryten Queen Tancorix to preserve the realm, no one doubted my ability." His voice fell and he added, "I spilled my blood across this entire world, Javan."

"And you bear the scars to prove it, sire. The known lands—and even some unknown—are marked with your footsteps."

"Indeed." He spoke with pride, but again, his voice fell. "So I journey to this place, this new land, out of boredom and perhaps…well…" Rogan's voice trailed off.

"Palace politics are not your strong suit," Javan said gently. "Prince Rohain is maturing into a role made for him. We all know that."

His uncle didn't reply. Javan looked to Captain Huxira to see if he noted the rough waters. The old Olmek-Tikalize man frowned, doing his best to steer the vessel from the rear.

Nodding, Rogan finally responded, gripping the handle of the broadsword attached to his heavy leather belt. "Rohain feels the wanderlust in his blood, too, but he seems more apt to deal with generals and politicians than I."

His attention returned to the sky.

"Your daughter Erin is a striking damsel and will make someone a fine bride," Javan said. "Young Teran is a powerful, if impetuous youth. Algeniz is a wonderful girl. All my cousins are blessed. There is much to be happy with in your life, sire."

"Happiness isn't all there is in life," Rogan brooded, squinting. The flock of birds was gone, leaving a single circling shadow, much larger than the others. "It's only a portion of it. Once one has done all and achieved so much, what is there when the blood still calls? What is there to yet be done? To be seen, tasted, and felt?"

"It is hard for you to handle contentment, sire?"

The seas grew choppier. Captain Huxira cursed, and several of the sailors mumbled in agreement.

"No matter how gentle your words, Javan," Rogan said, "yes, that is so."

"But you regret this adventure now?"

Rogan shrugged his bronzed shoulders and watched the giant bird as it drew closer.

"What a wingspan on that beast, it cuts an odd image, no? It reminds me of fetishes made to Damballah, a god of the dark continent across the sea to the south."

"Sire?"

Rogan shook his head as if to shake a memory loose. "Nothing—it's nothing, boy. Just an old adversary. What was I saying? Oh, yes. I seek not just an escapade, but something else. Something indefinable. After one grows to an age, one can feel the ebbing away of power and lusts. My mind is willing, but the body, well, it thinks about disgracing me."

Javan nodded, unsure of what to say.

Rogan glowered. "Don't think that of me, boy! I can still knock down a woman and claim her. I still awake each morning with timber beneath my loincloth. I just don't want to die in my bed, Javan. To die in bed, surrounded by weeping maidens? That's not the way for one such as me."

The waves grew stronger, lapping at the bireme. Several of the sailors had to grab on to the sides to keep from being thrown to the deck. They shouted in despair.

"Steady," Captain Huxira called. "The sea grows angry."

Rogan and Javan glanced at him, and then finished their conversation.

"You are a man born in Caucausia," Javan said. "None of your kin would want that either. But we don't know what the future holds. Perhaps seeing these grand sites will—"

Every breath on the bireme suddenly stopped as two reddish serpentine tentacles exploded from the choppy waves, thrusting up from the right and left sides. A half-dozen more tendrils quickly joined the scarlet appendages.

"Sea monster," Harkon shouted, drawing his steel. "To arms! Quickly!"

Wagnar stepped to his brother's side, sword at the ready. "I told you that fish was a bad omen. Now, Dagon sends another of his spawn!"

The slaves, still chained to their rowing posts, screamed in horror as the waters churned. Oars snapped like twigs in the creature's tentacles. The long red arms angrily slapped the craft, rocking it back and forth. Many of those standing were thrown to the deck. Arms flailing, Javan slammed into Rogan. They tumbled backward, collapsing in a tangled heap on the nose of the bireme. Rogan pushed the boy aside and stood. The waters foamed and then the main body of the creature surfaced off the right front side.

All of the men, young and old, Alatervaeian and Olmek-Tikalize, screamed.

All of them...except for Rogan.

Grinning, he spat into the wind. The monster would provide far more sport than the fish had.

"Come on, then," he challenged the beast.

Javan sprang to his feet, but the tentacles slammed into the bireme again. The youth nearly flipped over the edge, but Rogan grabbed the nape of his tunic and pulled him back.

"Fill your bow, Javan," Rogan snarled. He leapt into a crouch and barked at the crew. "Get your pikes and spears up here, Wodan damn you all!"

Amazed that the ship still ran level, Javan fought to gain his balance. He swallowed down the fear in his throat, unslung his bow, fixed two arrows and drew back, setting his eyes on the beast. All sound had ceased, save his pulse, throbbing in his ears. His heart beat like a rabbit. He hesitated, staring at the slender, tube-shaped head protruding from the beast's bulbous red torso. Two obsidian circles stared back.

"It looks like a banana," he sputtered, "or a gourd with eyes..."

Teeth clenched, Rogan grabbed a spear from a stunned sailor, reared back and threw it at the creature.

"Even a gourd with eyes still *has* eyes, boy! Let your aim find them."

Clearing his head, Javan drew in a breath and released. The steel tipped arrows sailed toward the main body of the beast, striking just as Rogan's spear deflected off an area between its eyes. A high-pitched screech ripped the air, not in pain, but rage. The creature's maw opened, side to side, like a split beak.

One elongated arm coiled around a young sailor and dragged the flailing victim below the surface. When the limb emerged from the water, the sailor's struggles had ceased and the body hung limp.

Lurching forward on the swaying deck, Harkon and Wagnar hurled spears at the monster. In response, one of its tendrils twisted around the handrails on the edge of the boat, snapping them like sticks. Wagnar buried his broadsword in the rubbery flesh. The steel sank deep into the tentacle, lodging in the middle. Pulpy fluid burst from the wound. Ichor ran across the deck and Harkon slipped on the boards, striking his head on the butt of an oar as he went down.

Rogan watched the beast try to reposition itself to the east side of the ship. Head swiveling, he assessed the situation, reverting to his days as a battlefield commander.

"You men, help me with the grapnels!"

The sailors obeyed Rogan's edict as the bireme went up on its left side, nearly capsizing. More appendages thudded from beneath the hull. Javan fired twice more at the eyes of the beast, missing again. He cursed his faulty aim.

"My father would hang his head in shame were he to see this display."

"Tis not your skills, young master," the toothless Captain Huxira advised him, stabbing a seeking tendril with his curved dagger. "Tis the pitching of this craft. Surely, the beast means to sink us."

Harkon and Wagnar's swords flashed up and down, glinting in the sunlight. The brothers fought as one. Gore and fluids covered them but they didn't seem to notice.

"Javan," Rogan called out, "to me."

Javan ran to his uncle's side, half sliding past him. "What have you in mind, sire?"

Rogan grabbed the long, heavy grapnels. "If that sea monster wants to hug us, by Wodan, he'll feel my embrace first. AWAY!"

They released the grapnels. The long cords took hold of several of the creature's squirming tentacles.

"Pull," Rogan implored all who could hear him.

A dozen men heaved on the lines.

Wagnar yelled, "Sire, we will flip over or be dragged down with it!"

"Nay!" Rogan bellowed as the bireme leveled out, using the force of the giant beast against it.

A few of the grapnels bit into the monster's appendages, severing them. The creature roared again, and several of the sailors clasped their ears. Enraged tentacles slapped at the men, crushing and twisting. One appendage coiled around a young sailor's midsection, squeezing him in half, letting his crushed upper half sag over, leaving legs to stand for a moment, not realizing they were dead. Another snaked over Huxira, but the old man stabbed it with his dagger and the tendril recoiled. The screams of a slave grew muffled as a tentacle wrapped around his head and flexed, crushing his skull like an overripe melon. His brains dripped from the arm as it sought out more prey. Still, he held his oar and stayed at his post.

The bireme lurched again and knocked Rogan to the deck. He slid across the ship and flipped over, almost going into the churning sea.

"Rogan!" Javan reached out for his uncle's hand as if he could breach the great distance for him.

"Stop crying, dammit," Rogan snapped as he got to his feet. A tentacle whipped by his head. He withdrew his broadsword and ordered, "Release the grapnels again."

The sailors released the grapnels and the beast's embrace slacked. It surged toward them again, long arms flailing, wrapping around the ship's hull.

As the bireme slanted, Rogan leapt past the cringing sailors. Sword held high up like a spear, he dropped onto the creature's head, right above its maw. The monster bellowed, infuriated at this intrusion.

"For Wodan!" he shouted, driving the blade deep into the beast's left eye, seeking a death stroke. The thing's screams increased as Rogan shoved the sword deeper, twisting as if he were planting fence posts. The hilt jutted from the head, and the creature shuddered. Using the wound as a foothold on the slippery hide, Rogan inserted a boot into the bloody gash and yanked his sword free. Stabbing down again, he probed for the brain. Finding none, he dodged the frenzied tendrils, still clinging to the monster's head.

A great cheer went up from the sailors. Javan shook his head from side to side.

Rogan used the beak of the monster as a stepping-stone, and crossed over; thrusting the blade into the beast's other eye. The creature heaved backwards with a tumultuous splash. One massive tentacle gripped Rogan's waist, dragging him beneath the waves. The creature submerged and all that was left was a mass of red foam.

The bireme rocked as the sailors ran to the side, desperate for a glimpse of their barbarian leader.

The red water's surface grew still.

"Oh goddess, no," Javan whispered.

Then, from the crow's nest high above their heads, a sailor shouted, "I see him!"

Rogan surfaced, spitting water and shaking his mane.

Captain Huxira laughed, shoving his men into action. "Throw him a line. The sharks will be out for a meal soon. The blood in the water calls to them. Hurry now."

Javan shuddered as Rogan was hauled back onboard. Sleek, angular shark fins already jutted from the water, racing towards them.

"That took a lot of stones," Harkon muttered.

"Or no brains," Wagnar whispered.

Tired, but defiant, Rogan chuckled. "Harkon. Wagnar. You boys are hardly alive. You haven't even seen your twenty-first summer yet. I have seen sixty of them. Never have I been more ready to die, yet felt more alive."

Javan found a dry cloak in the back of the ship and slipped it around Rogan's shoulders.

"Sire," Wagnar exclaimed, "never have I seen such a beast. Surely Dagon sent it to impede us?"

Saving his breath, Rogan shrugged.

"Or perhaps Leviathan," Harkon muttered.

The others blanched at the name, making the various signs of their own preferred deities. Rogan eschewed such religious nonsense, but even he turned grim at Leviathan's mention.

"Speak not of the Thirteen," Javan warned Harkon. "Lest you draw their attention. They have many doors into this world. To speak of them is to invite them entry."

Rogan spat over the side. "The Thirteen need no invitation, Javan. None of their kind does. If they want to come, let them come. I'll face them while the rest of you cower."

The crew fell silent.

Huxira grimaced. "This creature that attacked us was just that—a creature, rather than some demonic beastie. I have seen its like from afar, but they never come this close to shore. Methinks this attack wasn't chance. It was guided. We are lucky to have our lives."

"A guided beast?" Rogan laughed, but his response held no humor. "Oh, bullcrap."

Frowning, Javan looked up. Even after the battle, the huge lone bird still circled in the empty sky.

And now there was something *else* in the distance.

"Sire," he said. "Look."

Rogan squinted at the stern of the ship, shielding his eyes with his gore-streaked hands. "Ho! Crow's nest! What is that on the horizon?"

The sailor perched high above directed his viewing glass to where Rogan pointed. "Eyes of an eagle on you, my Lord. It's a ship!"

"I deduced that, you donkey's ass." Rogan spat, still getting his breath back. "Of what kind? Whose markings?"

The sailor concentrated and then looked down from his viewer. "Hard to say sir, but it is moving very fast. A large galley. There are no markings, no flag. I—" He raised his glass and looked in another direction. "Sire! Off port! Another ship, but much smaller."

"Get me a looking glass," Rogan ordered one of the sailors, who still appeared stunned from the fight with the sea monster. The young man swiftly vanished and then returned with a long viewer.

Rogan looked skyward and again saw the large bird. "What is that cursed thing up there, Javan?"

"At first I thought it an eagle, sire, but the tips of the wings point at strange angles like those of a bat."

"A bat? That size? Don't jerk me around."

Wagnar, Harkon, Javan, and Captain Huxira gathered around Rogan, watching the horizon with apprehension. The larger ship produced tiny ships off its sides as it sailed toward them.

Javan gasped. "It's a mother ship."

Huxira leaned forward, his breath reeking of chewing leaf.

"They are not of Olmek-Tikal. What are they, King Rogan?"

Rogan frowned at the title given him by the descendent of Atlantis. "The small vessels look like Pryten reavers. Notice the great speed they exhibit and the way they harness the wind with their short sails."

"Prytens?" Wagnar laughed. "Pirates? Those savages could in no way be here. Their lands lie halfway around the world."

Rogan's countenance grew grim. "Those fools would have the sack, but you're right. It wouldn't be possible for them to sail all this way."

With diplomacy, Javan said, "A Pryten reaver could survive the journey through these hostile waters if lashed to a larger ship."

Frowning, Rogan considered this. He raised his glass to the sky, seeking the bird again.

The man in the crow's nest called out, "They are coming right at us!"

Captain Huxira spat a wad of brown juice over the side of the damaged craft. "A few pirate bastards? They will be sorry to tangle with us. Fix bows!"

Harkon wiped the monster's sticky blood from his blade. "A few dozen Pryten savages will meet a harsh fate trying to board us. I'll send their balls back in memory of their dead Queen Tancorix to her daughter, Andraste."

Despite the losses incurred during the sea beast's attack, the bireme sported seventy men rowing, two-dozen sailors, the two Alatervaeian bodyguards, Javan, and Rogan.

As the ship took to battle stations and the sailors re-armed themselves with bows, the man in the crow's nest sang out, "They aren't Prytens!"

Again, Rogan raised his glass, muttering, "You wouldn't know a Pryten if you shat on one. Shut your fool mouth and abide by me." He focused on the men in the small vessels and his mind spun. "Donar's balls, he's right. They are blacks from the dark kingdoms."

Javan gripped his bow. "Those savages couldn't pilot such vessels so far away from home any better than a Pryten. It isn't possible."

"Unless they were hired, supplied, and helped. I was a pirate amongst men such as these on the Ebony Coast in my youth. Don't discount their abilities based solely on the color of their skin and the gods they worship. They are damned fierce warriors."

"I will take your word for it, sire."

"Then take my word for something else, as well. The captain was right. That assault by the sea monster wasn't random. Neither is this. We are under attack and it's anything but random."

"But who could orchestrate such a thing?"

"Who indeed? But the more important question is why."

"This is a transport ship we ride on," Javan insisted, "not a war vessel. Aside from the ram on the front, what defense do we have? They cannot think we have booty."

"Get it through your skull, boy. By Wodan, Javan, you may have General Thyssen's strength, but you think like a damned politician! Always believing the best in folk—bah—that doesn't even work on brats. The real world is a different place. Those men aren't after the ship or plunder. Thousands of miles from home, they are here on a purpose. I told you that flying creature above reminded me of Damballah?"

Javan nodded.

"These men are seeking a target. That's why that creature is circling us like a hungry buzzard. By magic or by stealth, *they want me and that bird has led them to us.*"

2 CLASH WITH THE CORSAIRS

THE DAMAGED BIREME listed to the port side as its inhabitants went to battle stations. Javan watched the sailors make quick work of the sails, while others brought up more weapons from the cabins below. Captain Huxira's men were no strangers to warfare on the open seas. They moved decisively and with astonishing speed, especially given the fact that several of them still bled from wounds suffered under the sea creature's recent attack. Bows, short swords, maces, pikes, and small forearm shields filtered amongst the men. Confusion and panic flashed on the sweaty faces of the rowing slaves, toiling under the taskmaster's persistent lash. Javan felt an unexpected flash of pity for them. His uncle would have chided him for the emotion, but this danger threatened the slaves, as well. Finally, his gaze came to rest on Rogan, still tall, sturdy, and imposing in his advanced years, seething under his wrinkled skin at the rapidly advancing smaller ships. His smile, wolflike, terrible to behold.

"How do they move so fast, Javan?" Wagnar asked, knuckles white on his pommel.

Javan affirmed, "Light sails. They maneuver well with little effort."

"Who sent them on to us, bound up to such a vessel?" Harkon asked.

Javan glanced to the circling bird and offered, "Who knows? It doesn't matter now, does it?"

Rogan nodded, clutching the handle of his broadsword, letting the heavy weight of it rest on side of the ship. "Aye, true enough. They'll be on us soon."

Captain Huxira barked orders in Olmek-Tikalize as the vessels sped towards them. The sailors all took a knee, partially concealing themselves behind the undamaged ridge of the boat and raised their large bows. The taskmaster cracked his whip and the slaves doubled their efforts on the oars.

Wagnar noticed the wet breeches of one of the sailors who had just come from the hold. He elbowed his brother.

"Either that man has soiled himself or we are taking on water."

"We're taking on water," Harkon confirmed. "We must send these dogs to their gods with haste, lest we all feed the sharks. We'll sink before long."

Javan looked up at Rogan. "You wanted a glorious death?"

Not looking back, Rogan snapped, "Shut your ass."

"On my word!" Captain Huxira shouted, and then paused, his eyes wide. "Look at them!"

The attackers were heavily muscled and black as coal; clad in little more than loincloths. Each bore hoops of gold and other decorations in their noses and ears. Ivory teeth flashed savage grins. The ebony warriors raised their bows, but unlike Captain Huxira's crew, didn't hesitate. They unleashed a volley of long, flaming arrows, and seconds later, crackling orange flames greedily engulfed the mast.

"Damn you, dogs," Rogan barked. "Release!"

The stunned crew unleashed their arrows, but a second volley was already soaring towards them. The sky rained feathered shafts, and sailors on both sides dropped to the decks.

Javan, crouching, noticed that even as the smaller boats strafed the bireme, the larger galley bore down on them.

Hefting a spear, Wagnar leaped over a wounded sailor and roared an Alatervaeian battle cry. Muscles and tendons stood taut, and he projected a ferocious image. Smoke from the burning sails obscured him for a moment.

When the smoke lifted, he lay jittering on the deck, a gray arrow jutting from his eye.

"Wagnar!"

Enraged, Harkon sprang to his brother's side. His huge hands cradled Wagnar's head. His brother's blood and brain matter oozed from around the arrow shaft and ran between his fingers.

"Brother," Harkon whispered. "You have left me here alone."

"Focus, Harkon." Javan coughed as the smoke reached him. "Make sure he did not die in vain."

Harkon raised his head and stared at the youth. His red-rimmed eyes burned with bloodlust and vengeance.

"I swear this to thee, Javan," he seethed. "These waters will run with their blood by the time this day is done. My brother shall be avenged."

"Then, for Rogan—and for your brother, make it so."

The fires raced up the mast. The smoke grew thick.

"Captain," Rogan commanded, "get some men on those flames. Quickly, now!"

Huxira panicked. "They are already below, bailing the seawater rushing through the hull. I'll have some others to attend to it."

A spear slammed into the boards at the old man's feet. Captain Huxira scrambled backward. Rogan yanked the spear out and hurled it back at the warrior who'd thrown it. The shaft buried itself in the man's chest, and he toppled into the water. Rogan spied another small boat approaching on a collision course from the north. The grinning pilot didn't turn or slacken his pace. Cursing, Rogan grabbed Javan and wrestled him to the other side of the vessel as the Pryten reaver rammed into them.

The black men on board the reaver leapt into the air with cat-like grace. A dozen of them boarded the vessel, swinging great curved swords and hiding behind long, oval-shaped bronze shields. The bireme tilted and swayed from the blow to its side. Below decks came the sounds of cracking timbers and bones, and the screams of the dying.

"They are well trained," Rogan observed, picking up a bow from a fallen archer.

One of the pirates hacked the head from a sailor. He raised his eyes and glared at Rogan, just in time to have an arrow sprout from his throat.

Quarters were too close to reload the bow, so Rogan swung the shaft up, snapping it off on the jawbone of an attacker. Trying to unsheathe his sword, Rogan needed more time as another man came after him. He seized the fighter's nipple ring and yanked it from the dark flesh. The wounded savage wailed in agony, allowing Rogan to free his blade.

Javan drew his small sword as well, throwing an elbow into the spine of Rogan's new opponent. Nearby, Harkon raved, swinging his sword in wild, sweeping arcs as the berserker bloodlust seized him. With each pirate's head he sent spinning into the frothing waters, he shouted his brother's name. The element of surprise was against the bireme's crew, and the corsairs had the upper hand, but Rogan, Javan, and Harkon killed a dozen of the attackers in an instant. They swung hard with their heavy weapons, splitting shields and skulls. Heads and limbs dropped from torsos, and blood jetted across the wet boards.

Another Pryten crept towards Captain Huxira. The pirate's gold earrings glinted in the sun. He thrust his spear forward, but the old man dodged the attack and lashed out with his dagger, slicing the black man's abdomen. The corsair drew back, and Huxira plunged the dagger into his side. The blade scraped against the man's ribs. Whispering rumors of the Pryten's mother's heritage and how she'd mated with a goat, Captain Huxira twisted the dagger and opened his opponent up. As the Pryten died, the old man spat a wad of chewing leaf into his face. Then he reached for a leather pouch and stuffed more leaf into his mouth with bloodstained fingers.

The bireme listed farther to port. Racing flames licked at the fluttering sails. Billowing smoke filled the air. Several crewmen struggled to extinguish the fires. They scaled the burning mast and were shot down with arrows from the bowmen aboard the Pryten mothership.

Rogan slipped in a steaming pile of intestines loosed from the belly of another pirate, parrying a sword blow as he collapsed to one knee. Face to face with black legs, he hacked the ankles from his target in a clean swipe. The man toppled over.

With one vicious thrust, Harkon impaled two of the savages as they rushed him. He smashed a third man's face with his shield, watching the pirate's nose burst like ripe fruit, before retrieving his sword.

"My brother will meet you on the other side, dog." Harkon skewered the man with his blade.

Javan felt a kick from behind as he slashed a throat. His opponent's jugular vein sprayed blood. Falling to his knees, Javan turned and drove his blade into the groin of the second warrior. The man collapsed to the slick deck, a small whine escaping from his frothing lips. Javan yanked his weapon free and the wounded savage curled into a ball, hands cradling his flayed manhood.

As the mothership turned sideways in front of the bireme, Captain Huxira shouted more commands. He aimed the listing bireme at the long ship, even as he took an arrow in the shoulder. Grimacing, he snapped the shaft, spat another wad of chewing leaf, and continued his efforts.

Another corsair, so dark that the sunlight seemed to reflect off his skin, and taller than even Rogan, stood in the long aisle between the terrified rowing slaves. He laughed, tossing his beaded locks of hair as a second Pryten reaver crashed into the bireme, depositing a dozen more warriors.

This time, they didn't attack the sailors, but swung weapons at the chains imprisoning the rowers.

In moments, a dozen slaves were free. The pirates boarding the bireme handed them small dirks, and encouraged them to join in the fight against their oppressors. The slaves clambered to their feet, cheering their newfound saviors.

Rogan stepped forward.

"Back, you worthless fools," he shouted in Albion, decapitating two of his own slaves in the hope of quelling the rebellion before it began.

The Pryten savage with the long, beaded hair laughed at him.

"Laugh now, mutt." Rogan pointed his blade at the pirate. "For soon, you'll only shriek."

Rogan, Javan, Harkon, and two of Huxira's sailors waded into the corsairs, slicing and stabbing, swinging and cutting for all they were worth. Huxira's men were slashed to ribbons. Harkon and Javan leapt over their corpses. Consumed with fury, Rogan tried to reach the giant Pryten leader, who freed more slaves. Bodies fell into the ocean and more shark fins appeared as if by magic. The churning water turned red. The roar of warfare, the clash of steel, and the cries for freedom from the slaves rang in the air.

A rock-hard fist struck Javan in the temple, the blow knocking him to his knees again. The boy's ears rang. The battle's din became a slight buzz. He shook his head, trying to clear it, as a pirate hovered over him. The attacker raised his sword and brought it sweeping down, but Harkon parried the deathblow with a stolen spear. The bodyguard ripped the corsair's sword from his hands and then thrust it back into the man's belly. The pirate tottered backward in surprise, clutching the hilt. One of the bireme's crewmen cleaved the wounded Pryten savage in half. Harkon nodded at the sailor. The sailor nodded back. Then Harkon helped Javan to his feet and danced away, consumed once more with bloodlust.

The fires continued devouring the masts. The sails were fluttering sheets of flame. Only the main mast, with the crow's nest at its top, remained unscathed. Despite the smoke and fire, Captain Huxira's crew managed to fend off the pirates' and slaves' combined onslaught and stood their ground. Just as they thought the worst neared an end, the sailor in the crow's nest shouted that more reavers were coming. Having drawn his attention, the leader of the corsairs threw a spear at the lookout. The missile impaled the sailor's foot, and he plummeted from his perch. He slammed against the oars on the eastern side of the ship. One of the slaves tossed him over the side, into the waiting jaws of the sharks. The sea foam, normally white, turned pink hued. The rest of the freed slaves advanced on the bireme's crew.

The vessel's hull splintered on the aft section as more pirates boarded. Captain Huxira, still driving the shattered, flaming bireme toward the Pryten galley despite his injured arm, let go of the wheel for a second and swung a long sword, slaying two men before they skewered him on their spears. Then he grabbed the wheel again. Harkon and three crewmembers sprang to his aide, fighting valiantly, but were soon overwhelmed. Javan caught a quick glimpse of Harkon's intestines slipping from a wound in his belly, and then the big man was crushed beneath more savages.

Captain Huxira closed his eyes and whispered a prayer to his god.

Javan closed his eyes as well, and held on for dear life.

Rogan was oblivious, the heat of battle consuming him. He killed slave and pirate alike, not wanting those still in bondage to join the growing throng of opposition.

The bireme slammed into the larger ship, ripping a hole in its side. Both the crewmembers and corsairs alike were mangled in the crash. The burning bireme rolled over, spilling the remaining inhabitants into the ocean. The sharks swarmed. Those slaves still in chains were eaten like dangling bait.

Treading water and clutching his sword, Javan searched for his uncle. A floating barrel of apples bumped into him, followed by a severed leg.

"Rogan?" he yelled. "Sire?"

There was no response. A wave crashed over him, obscuring his vision. Choking on bloody saltwater, Javan shouted again.

"Uncle?"

Something hard brushed against his boot. At first, he thought it was another barrel, but when he looked down, he saw a sleek, gray form beneath the surface. Javan held still, waiting for the shark to pass. Floating amongst the blood and body parts, he saw the mothership taking on water. Then he heard a savage cry.

Javan gasped, his eyes staring in disbelief.

Rogan rode the capsized bireme like a steed. He stood with his feet apart and his sword ready. The towering leader of the corsairs faced him, brandishing a curved blade. His beaded locks of hair matted with the blood of those he'd slain.

"You are finished," Rogan roared, jabbing his broadsword at the great ship taking on water. "Your transport sinks to the bottom of these waters, and you shall join it momentarily."

"My life matters not," the pirate responded in the Albion language. "We were sent to make sure you die, old man. I have done my job."

"Sent by whom?"

The black warrior looked up to the sky, pursed his lips at the giant bird, and then faced Rogan again. "That matters not, as well. We were sent to kill you. Under the blessings of Damballah, we have attained that. He will be happy for the blood spilled this day."

Treading water, Javan reached the overturned bireme. Neither his uncle nor the black warrior noticed. A shark loomed beneath him, but then darted off to consume a floating, mangled corpse.

"I spit in Damballah's face," Rogan laughed. "Call your little god down and let him taste the wrath of one given life by Wodan."

The leader grinned, tossing his curved blade from hand to hand. "Damballah smiles upon us, old man, for your death is assured. But before I let loose your entrails, since you asked—take this knowledge to your watery grave. In your kingdom of Albion, a true heir will soon rise to the throne. The first born of your loins is not Rohain, but Karac, whom you sired with a Nubian concubine of Zimbabwe."

Javan gripped the side of the bireme and shook his head in disbelief. Another shark brushed by him, but he barely noticed.

Rogan blinked. "You speak madness! I haven't bedded a black woman since before I wed Desna, my Queen. That was decades ago."

"Indeed it was. Yet her son is the rightful heir to your seat. Even now, Karac moves to assassinate young King Rohain, and to bed your daughter, and to take what is rightfully his."

"What's your name, dog?" Rogan snarled; his forearms flexing as his grip tightened on his sword handle. "I would know before I feast on your heart."

"I am Karac's younger brother," the man grinned. "My name is Karza. I am the one who is about to take your life. I am also a product of your loins."

Eyes narrow, Rogan hissed, "You lie."

"Try me and see...*father*."

Rogan charged Karza. The warrior fought well, easily deflecting Rogan's wild, angered blows. The black man was no simple pirate, but properly trained in the methods of physical combat. He warded off the old man and then kicked him in the stomach. Stumbling backward, Rogan crashed to the splintered deck. His breath whooshed from his lungs. Laughing, Karza thrust at him, but Rogan lashed out, forcing him back.

As Rogan rose up and charged his opponent again, Javan pushed himself out of the water and onto the boat. Swords clashed, echoing above the screams of the sharks' unfortunate victims.

Javan knew that while his uncle's fighting ability looked deadlier than ever, his stamina would eventually wane. Karza obviously understood this as well, and played the older warrior for time. They locked together in a dance, stabbing and parrying, thrusting and kicking. Karza's fist crashed into the side of Rogan's head. Rogan spun away, sucking in salty air and narrowly avoiding the curved blade.

Javan glanced down at the water. The upper half of Captain Huxira's lifeless body bobbed on the surface. The old man's cheek still bulged with a wad of chewing leaf. Javan reached out and closed Huxira's eyes. Then he seized a floating bow. He had three arrows left in his quiver. Removing two, he snapped them down onto the cord of the bow and drew back.

"Goddess," he prayed, "guide my hand."

He loosed the missiles. Both arrows struck Karza in the back, below his shoulder blades, impaling his lungs—just as General Thyssen had taught Javan to do.

Staggering forward, Karza raised his sword. Blood spewed from his mouth as he coughed. Rogan renewed his attack. There was little power behind the corsair's defense as Rogan slapped the curved blade down and raised his weapon again. The heavy broadsword bit into Karza's shoulder, and both the curved sword and the arm that held it fell into the water.

Karza screamed.

Rogan laughed. "Some son of mine you are, must've been from what was left on the mattress."

Javan expected Rogan to hesitate at slaying one of his own bastard children, but he did not. With a guttural curse, Rogan grasped Karza's beaded hair and removed the pirate's head, sawing through flesh and bone, slow. Half dead from the arrows, Javan wondered if Karza felt the sawing action meant to torture him before death. Rogan kicked the corpse into the sea and held the head aloft, bellowing with rage before flinging it to the sharks as well. There was a splash, and then Karza's head rolled upright, bobbing on the surface and staring at them with glassy eyes.

Panting for breath, Rogan crouched on the floating timbers, staring at his opponent's face. Despite the warrior's black skin, their profiles were the same.

"He'll soon sleep in a shark's belly." Rogan looked to the horizon.

"He claimed you were his father," Javan murmured, sucking wind.

"If he was a product of my loins…" Rogan shrugged, still watching the horizon. "Every man can have an off night, Javan."

The great mother vessel sank fast and Javan picked off a pirate trying to swim to them for salvation. Then he fished arrows out of the water to re-supply his quiver.

Two more pirates tried to board them. Rogan kicked both back into the shark-infested drink. One of Huxira's men grasped the side, but before Javan could pull him aboard, a shark pulled the helpless man beneath the surface.

"When the night swells come up," Rogan said calmly as a deathly quiet started to settle in, "we are surely lost on this hulk."

"Pray, sire."

Rogan frowned and stared again to the East. "I should have stayed a pirate myself."

Yet another hand arose over the side of the smashed hulk. Casually, Rogan chopped off the fingers and the body fell into the waters with a muffled cry.

Shielding his eyes from the waning sun, Javan looked west in the direction of their destination. "Perhaps we will make landfall, Rogan. We can't be too far off from shore."

Rogan's brooding blue eyes glared at the bloody smears on the boards. "What if we do, boy? Does it matter? This

Karac sent his brother after us. He wanted me dead so that I couldn't come back seeking revenge or to reclaim the crown. So what if we make landfall? Can you row a hundred oars and return us to the coast of Transalpina or the northern way to our allies in Thule? Nay. We are lost."

He paused.

"And if this dog, Karza, spoke true, then our loved ones are lost as well."

3 MISTY NEW WORLD

ROGAN KEPT HIS eyes closed, listening to the seagulls shrieking above, feeling the ruined vessel rock gently on the waves. Then he knew no more, until—

"Uncle," Javan shouted with exuberance. "We live still!"

Rogan lay adhered to the hull in a dried circle of blood, seawater, and sweat. The ocean lapped against the shattered craft, and the prolonged rhythm had lulled him to sleep. Rubbing his eyes and scratching at his salt-hardened beard, Rogan raised his head and blinked. He licked his sun-blistered lips and winced, grinning at the pain.

"You're a brilliant advisor after all, Javan. It's not a wonder I brought you along to interpret and counsel me. Of course we still live."

Javan's ears turned red. Feeling silly for his comment, he pointed.

"But look, sire."

Then he jumped into the blue-green water, which Rogan realized was free of blood and bodies.

"Javan? What madness has seized you?"

The brash action startled Rogan, and he arose quickly to see what had inspired his nephew's folly. Javan hopped in waist deep water, gesturing at the brown sandy beach nearby.

"We made it, sire." The boy laughed, splashing playfully. "Wodan is merciful. Rhiannon is just."

Rogan chewed salt from his mustache and stared at the shore. He slid into the cool water, his muscles aching, his wounds burning.

"Wodan is merciful? Mule shit. Wodan is a bitch's son with a bad sense of humor, boy. I may pray to your goddess, Rhiannon, before this day is out, instead."

Javan splashed again, then sank beneath the waves and emerged, spraying a mouthful of water.

"Javan, you're acting like a child. Do you still suckle at your mother's tit?"

The younger man ignored Rogan's sarcastic jab. His happiness to have survived the ordeal was etched in his expression.

"Sire, I know that you have cheated death many times in your life. It's an old cloak for you to discard, slipping out of the shadows of the afterlife. But this was my first true test. I hope this is the only time I must dodge such a foe."

"I've never cheated death, lad. I've only escaped him for a time."

"Still, I hope to never have to do the same again."

"All men meet death sooner or later, Javan. The trick is to bend him to your will. That's what I have always done. Nothing more. But my will is strong."

They waded ashore and collapsed in the warm, sun-baked sand. It stuck to their wounds and their raw skin, scratching and scraping—but neither had ever felt something more luxuriant. Gulls darted across the beach, their beaks snapping at small, scuttling crabs. Scrub grass swayed in the breeze and bleached driftwood dotted the dunes. Further inland, a dense forest walled off an immense series of mist-enshrouded mountains. The blue sky brushed against the mountaintops.

Rogan gazed up at the dwarfing spectacle.

Aye, my will is strong, he thought. *But death only can be bent over so many times. And as I get slower, his pace stays the same. Eventually, death comes for all.*

They sat in silence for a while, each lost in thought. The surf's lullaby washed over them.

"It is beautiful, this land," Javan breathed, spellbound. "The greenery is like an ocean itself. Look at the shafts of light from the sky, how they crease the mists wreathing the mountaintops."

Rogan nodded. "It almost makes one believe in the gods, eh?"

Javan frowned, ignoring his uncle's blasphemous words. "Look how far the coast goes on."

Rogan stretched, his sword dangling over his bare thigh. His blue eyes looked both ways and then back at the bireme's carcass.

"I'd kill for even a gelding mount now. Damned trees are probably full of Troglodytes like in the Pryten wilderness."

"Oh, I doubt that, sire."

"At least that cursed bird no longer hangs over us."

Javan gazed upward, shielding his eyes from the sun's glare.

"Do you really think that thing had some importance to our plight?"

"Yes," Rogan spat. "By the ass of the goddess, it was unnatural, and I felt the darkness in my bones. Think, lad. It was far too easy for them to find us in the middle of this unexplored and uncharted land. That last warrior, Karza—"

"The one who claimed to be your son?"

Rogan's face tightened. "He boasted of aide from the dark lord, Damballah. By Wodan and Rhiannon, they invoked *Damballah*."

Javan stood up, brushed the sand from his skin, and walked farther ashore. Rogan remained on the ground, letting the tide lap at him.

"Sire, I've heard of this god of the black peoples and read of him. I know you encountered their wizards before, when Rohain was abducted years ago."

"He ain't the god ya wanna fuck with."

"But I've never heard of Damballah making an actual appearance, except in the minds of the dark folk."

"Or in the nightmares of those in the north." Rogan took a deep breath. "I have dreamt of dark Damballah and the evil shade over Albion even now, on that blood-strewn deck, whilst you kept watch. This Karac, my bastard son they spoke of, is a true barbarian fighter. This wasn't the first I'd heard his name, though it was indeed news that he sprang from my loins. They say he is far more apt to the ways of war and bloodletting than most men. Perhaps even more than…" Rogan's voice faded, never saying the word—*Rohain.*

"My father and many others trained Rohain well, sire. Truly, this is a fancy story made up by these fools."

Rogan closed his eyes, lost in a fleeting vision.

"But I saw it in my dreams, how Karac planned it all, how he and his followers overthrew the palace by posing as slaves and teamsters." The old man's eyes popped open. "Perhaps it's all a nightmare brought on by my fear, aye? Let us try and ground her."

Javan gave him a confused look. "What?"

"That forest that so enthralls you isn't our most pressing matter, Javan. We must make camp. When we don't return, our friends in Olmek-Tikal may come to our aid. At the very least, they shall send a search party to find news of their missing loved ones. Let us try and flip this damaged hulk over. Perhaps we can ground her well and take shelter in her belly for the night."

This task was easier said than done. Leading the damaged vessel to shore was a great labor even in the shallow water, but flipping it over proved impossible, despite Rogan's strength. They dragged the long ship only a few feet before the ruined mast pole and other materials underneath sank into the wet sand.

Out of breath, Rogan fell on the dry part of the beach. As the breeze washed over them, he said, "The damned sea will take her back with the tides."

"Perhaps it will be shoved further ashore by the tides or sink in deeper, sire."

"Always looking on the dazzling side, eh, lad?" Rogan grinned.

"Well, Rhiannon is a god of light."

Rogan waved him off and looked to the mountains. "What manner of land is this, I wonder? Southern Olmek-Tikal was all full of swamps, marshes, and alligators when we sailed along its coast last year."

"Not an enjoyable journey, if my mind is sharp, sire." Javan's voice dripped with sarcasm. "I've no desire to repeat it."

"Since I saved you from quicksand on two different occasions, I can see why. This northern land looks much like the Corinthian mountains, does it not?"

"Indeed. It reminded me of them, too, Uncle. Such gigantic pines; they'd make an artist randy."

"Damned if I forgot my paints," Rogan grunted. "Still, scavenge what you can from the beach. It looks as though the seas don't want items that went to the bottom. We will need all we can if there is life here."

"Surely the cache of weapons in the rear chamber is intact? If I swim under the ship, perhaps I can retrieve them."

Approving this idea, Rogan waded back into the water, and waited. Piece by piece Javan retrieved armor and weapons from the rear of the boat, which was still underwater. The youth then tossed them to Rogan, who carried each item to shore. He was stunned at how many times Javan dived and returned with knives or swords.

At last, Rogan called, "Do you need to breathe, boy?"

Javan winked and dove again. This time he returned with a blade in his teeth and a round shield in his left hand. In his right hand was a bottle of wine. Rogan grabbed the bottle and his perpetual scowl gave way to a slight smile.

"You see?" Javan laughed. "Just what we needed."

Rogan unsealed the canister of wine and said, "We?

Dive again for your own." He waited until the youth was underwater, and then mumbled, "I swear, the boy is half fish."

They carried the weapons and water flasks up the beach. Rogan drank deeply from the wine while Javan heaped the weapons in a grassy area out of the reach of the surf.

Rogan sat down and looked back at the water. The alcohol coursed through his veins, easing his pain.

Javan pointed at the sea birds and crabs. "At least there is wildlife in abundance. And I found a fishing rod amidst the weapons."

"Wonderful. So we'll not starve right away."

Rogan squinted at the sky. In the distance, he thought he saw the bat-winged bird again, but when he blinked it was gone. He cursed his fading senses, disregarding it as a trick of his mind, brought on by exhaustion and the wine.

"We will only have to survive a brief time, sire. Surely, you are correct and others from the southern part of Olmek-Tikal will search for us when we do not return!"

Rogan shrugged, nostrils testing the sea air. "Probably. If they find us it'll be a miracle all in itself. We traveled a long way. They may give up in despair before ever reaching this point."

"The natives in Olmek-Tikal practically worship you," Javan reminded him. "They would not desert you any more than I would."

Brooding, Rogan drank more wine. "Perhaps. We'll just have to wait and see. They may be happy to be rid of their white king. Bah—I've grown tired of such primitive ignorance, anyway. I came here for adventure, not to be a god to a pack of red-skinned farmers and fishermen."

"They will send others if we do not return, sire. I am positive."

Rogan spat, eyes to the ocean.

Javan paused. "Uncle, may I speak freely?"

Rogan rinsed his mouth with wine and spat it onto the sand.

"Speak."

"I feel that your mind is on what Karza said was transpiring in Albion."

"Damned genius, you are. Of course, boy. The thought that my eldest son is dead and my kin suffer under the damned heel of southern invaders—by Wodan...that's hard to swallow. How could bright Albion fall so? It isn't as if they could sneak up with legions of troops." Eyes closed, he saw the dream images of the black teamsters by the grand palace in Albion and his joints ached anew.

Javan took up a bow and a single arrow. "But sire, even if we turned the bireme back over we could hardly sail back to the port of Argos in her. She barely floats, after the assault from both the creature and the corsairs. Such open seas would swamp us. It is a gift from above that we survived the night swells."

Rogan again gazed to the sky. "That's why we hugged the continent and rode it out slow to land. Woe as I am to admit it, our foes found us, half a world away, with the power of Damballah. There's no other explanation."

Javan stooped, smelling a patch of flowers blooming from a dune. "The bird-thing was an eye in the sky for a wizard?"

"Perhaps."

"You certainly have no love for magic."

"Stupid men allow their fears to be made large by wizards, Javan. Consider our companions from Olmek-Tikal. They took beating hearts out of living men for their gods."

"Until we stopped them," Javan said, "and taught them another way."

"I think all wizards tend to cavort with minions in darkness because no woman will have them."

Javan laughed at the jest. "That doesn't make them any less powerful."

"True. But they bleed just like any other man. I wonder about that bird we saw. It was unnatural—but not an illusion or some parlor trick. It looked like the stone idols of Damballah I saw as a younger man. And Karza said it served them."

Javan cleared his throat, inspecting the leaves of a squat bush. A swarm of angry gnats arose from the branches and pestered him. His uncle's words weighed heavily on him. Would they be forgotten, abandoned here on this forsaken beach?

"I hope the Olmek-Tikalize sailors come after us. If they do not…"

He choked down the words, not wanting his voice to betray the fear he felt inside.

"Welcome home, Javan," Rogan swept his hand toward the forest. "I bet that when Thyssen sent you along for maturing, he never dreamed that you'd be shipwrecked with his old king, eh?"

Javan shrugged and drew the string of his bow back. With one shot, he struck a swooping ivory-colored seagull. Squawking, it flopped in the water, and the young man ran into the surf to retrieve his prize, carefully avoiding the body parts of their fellow sailors that were beginning to wash ashore.

"At least you aren't skittish," Rogan hollered. "That surf is now thick with pieces of our foes or friends. Look how the sand is littered with their limbs, in just the brief time we've been ashore. We can't stay here the night, this will soon smell worse than ass."

Emerging from the water, Javan said, "Sire, I think you complimented me."

Rogan smiled. "Engrave it in stone, boy. It may be my only testament in such a manner to you."

A sudden gust of wind blasted off the ocean. Beyond the trees, they heard a deep growl. It didn't sound human. It did sound hungry. Exchanging glances, both men took to the bushes and hid, waiting.

Out of the trees lumbered a gigantic black bear. As the sea gave up the fruits of their awful triumph over the corsairs, the grisly bits of humanity along the shoreline tempted the animal. It sniffed the air and slowly padded onto the beach, devouring morsels here and there.

"What a beast," Rogan whispered. Javan had to strain to hear him. "This animal may be just what we need."

"What say you, sire?"

"Look to that mountain range. Such conditions remind me of the peaks south of Turana, not just Corithina. I would guess the temperature drops here at night and in the higher elevations."

"That is logical."

"Of course, it's damned logical. That bear's coat is thicker than the current late summer season in Albion. Perhaps we are farther north than we thought. He grows it not for a coming winter, but for everyday warmth. Since the sea has stripped us down to our loins, the choice is obvious. We must take him for his hide. It will keep us warm."

The bear raised its head, and looked around. Then it continued rooting. Its snout was crimson, and its long, pink tongue licked at the droplets of blood.

"How long since you last slain a bear single-handed, sire?"

Rogan shrugged. "I cannot recall. But I'm not hollowed out just yet. Besides, I have you along. Why should I fear him with your bow at my side?"

Javan breathed a heavy sigh and prepared. "I appreciate your faith, sire."

"Use the heavy arrows Karza's warriors had." Rogan rooted in the pile of weapons. "The forked heads are a work of savage art. Those pricks knew what they were doing."

"As you command."

"We have collected enough of those from the stray quivers on the beach. Wodan knows what else will vomit onto the shore over time. With a good chance we can pierce a lung in that hulk."

"I will do my best, lord."

"Keep firing if he doesn't go down." Rogan squeezed the handle of a double-headed battle-axe they'd retrieved from the bireme's mooring links. "I shall do the rest."

Javan mumbled a prayer to Rhiannon and stealthily positioned himself farther down the line of bushes. Rogan ran down the beach in the open for a few yards. The bear looked up from a rib cage that had washed ashore. It spied the old man clearly, but made no effort to follow. It had no fear, and no desire to hunt, since easier pickings lay at its feet. Instead, the beast lowered its snout and continued licking the scraps of organs and tissue still clinging to the bones.

Javan fired the first of his arrows into the bear's side. The beast grunted and then roared. Quickly, Javan drew from the quiver on his back and fired three more times, striking the creature in the side, close to the front quarters, and then the low-hanging belly. He expected the bear to drop, but instead, it stood firm.

Rogan loped further out onto the sand with the smooth ease of a tiger and fired his own long bow twice. The first shot missed, but the second arrow struck the bear deep in the other flank. The beast rose up, teeth bared as it howled. Thick flecks of foamy saliva dropped from its jowls.

Feet planted, Rogan let the bow slide from his fingers, and drew back, hefting the double-edged battle-axe. He roared in answer to the bear's challenge. The animal paused, uncertain of what it faced. Grunting hard, Rogan flung the heavy axe with all of his might. The weapon tumbled end over end, and buried itself under the beast's open maw, cleaving its jaws.

Staggering, the bear rocked back and forth on unsteady paws, but still refused to fall. Rogan drew his broadsword and charged low, like a bull. The mortally wounded animal tried to roar, but only a weak gurgle issued from its throat. Rogan avoided the desperate claws and stabbed his blade into the bear's abdomen. Going to all fours, the beast lurched a few steps, handle of the axe impacting on the ground, driving the blade in farther. It shuddered before collapsing. Rogan danced away again, inadvertently stomping on the leg of some partially eaten shark victim.

The bear shook, and then moved no more.

Rogan dropped to his knees and then rolled onto his buttocks beside it. He greedily sucked the salty air into his burning lungs.

Javan ran up, whooping in joy. "I think that axe head found its brain!"

Rogan eyed the boy and said, "I suppose you expect me to gut and clean him as well?"

Javan smiled. "It *is* your kill, Uncle."

"I'll clout you for that," Rogan promised. "But first I must rest."

It took them the rest of the day to skin and clean the bear, and it was dusk by the time they were finished. They washed their hands in the ocean, cleaning them of the sticky blood. They moved on down the way a piece, and then Javan started a fire behind a dune to prepare dinner. The meat gleaned from the kill ran tough and gamy. Gulls darted over their heads, begging for scraps. Rogan growled at them, and the shrieking scavengers fled into the night.

As they ate, Javan eyed the skeleton of the bireme in the distance.

"I was correct, sire. The ship is deeper in the sand now and will not be sucked out to sea."

"If we ever see Albion again," Rogan said around a mouthful of half-cooked bear flesh, "I shall have Rohain give you a medal. After we've defeated my bastard son's plot against him, of course."

"We will get back, sire. Some way, some how, we will."

Rogan shrugged, sucking the marrow from a bone. "Perhaps my destiny is to die here."

"Banish such thoughts, sire!"

The fire popped, sending a brief shower of burning embers into the night sky.

"If it is my time to die, you get to watch. Your father

would say it is a grand joke of fate, eh?"

Javan tilted his head to one side. "My father would never give in to fate."

Rogan nodded, thinking on old Thyssen and their adventures as revolutionaries. His smile was faint. Old ghosts danced in the flickering firelight. The night of a thousand knives. The whore with three breasts and the secret she'd told in the dark.

"True. You are young. You have space in your gut for fighting fate. My belly has wrestled that demon-whore for eons. She is a tireless bitch and I grow weary of her."

"I am not ready to die."

"No man ever is," Rogan replied. "Yes, you can cheat death, but you can never be ready for it. Think of Wagnar and Harkon. Or Captain Huxira—old as he was, I dare say he was not ready to die. When death comes, it comes. All that you can do is to meet it."

The fire crackled again. A second later, a twig snapped in response. Both men were instantly on their feet. The hair on Javan's arms stood up. Rogan tensed, alert and ready for whatever new danger lay in store.

Javan pointed to the bushes, suddenly alive with creeping shadows.

"Uncle—look!"

The shadows detached themselves from the bushes, and a group of humans stepped forward, just outside the circle of light. They were slender, clad in tan loincloths and deerskin cloaks. The strangers carried wooden staffs with tied stone spearheads, and several sported bows of a style that neither Rogan nor Javan had ever seen before. The flames flickered off their dense, ruddy complexions and red-tinged skin. Their obsidian hair shone in the moonlight as if their flat manes were slick and wet.

"Javan," Rogan ordered, "your bow."

But the weapon was already in the boy's hands.

Silently, the group stepped into the dying firelight. A few of the natives bore odd deformities; elongated heads, misshapen ears, one limb longer than another, even bizarre double noses. None made a move to attack. They seemed docile and curious. None of them spoke.

Another figure emerged, dressed in the skins of a gray wolf, the snout and muzzle still intact over his wrinkled forehead. The wolf-man's eyes glistened in the darkness, and Rogan surmised that his difference in dress made him a leader of some sort.

The odd individual held out his arms, showing the two strangers what he held: The gray, ropy intestines of the dead bear. Flies buzzed around them.

Javan's nose wrinkled in disgust at the slaughterhouse stench wafting off the guts. Slowly, he raised his bow, counting their numbers and wondering about the strength and reach of their spears.

Rogan drew his broadsword, gripping the handle so tightly that his sunburned knuckles turned white.

"Javan?"

"Yes, sire?"

"Speak to me again of fate, when we are done here."

The moon rose higher, bathing them in its cold light. Another log popped on the fire, sending more embers spiraling into the air. Nobody moved. Somewhere in the darkness, a whippoorwill cried out.

When he was a child, Javan's nursemaid had told him that when one heard the song of a whippoorwill, it meant that someone was about to die. Rogan's words rang in his head.

When death comes, it comes. All that you can do is to meet it.

As the wolf-headed leader stepped closer, Javan shivered.

Rogan thought of home, and his children.

4 TOTEMS, VISIONS, AND THE DEAD SHALL RISE

THE LEADER HELD forth his grisly offering but remained still, even when the halo of flies moved from the intestines to his wolf's head crown. He seemed to be awaiting a response from Rogan and Javan. When it became clear that none was forthcoming, he finally spoke, chattering to his companions.

Rogan frowned. "What in the name of Wodan is he saying?"

Javan, a master interpreter of most known languages because of his studies in Albion's famed university, concentrated on the speech patterns.

"They do not appear angry, but I cannot pick it up, sire. It is a strange tongue. Give me time."

"We don't have time. I think they deceive us. The wolf-headed fellow holds the guts of the bear the way a midwife holds a new babe. With my luck, I probably killed his accursed god."

"I don't think so. Look at his body language, the way he holds himself. He is not angry with us. Indeed, he seems to be trying to communicate."

"My eyes and my wits aren't dull. Of course he's trying to communicate. The question is; what do they want? Be they friend or foe?"

Cautiously, Javan motioned to the leader. "By his vestments, headdress, and voice inflection, I'd say he is their leader or perhaps their priest."

The old man babbled emphatically, as if he'd understood the youth. Javan tried other dialects. After a few moments, he grew excited.

"It is amazing, Uncle Rogan. I believe they speak a bastardized form of the language of those in northern Hyrcania. It's almost like a lost dialect I read of in class used only in Anthelia! I know it only because my teachers made such jest of the lingo."

Rogan remained silent but vigilant as Javan struggled to talk to the natives in this tongue. The red-skinned men seemed to understand him, at least partially. Several smiled, revealing jagged teeth. Then one of them laughed. Javan grinned as well.

"Do you understand them, boy?"

"I do, sire."

"Good. Now they can tell us for certain if we killed their god."

Javan shook his head. "No, I was correct. The man wearing the wolf's head is their priest or wizard. He calls himself a—shaman."

"Wizard. Shaman. It makes no difference." Rogan's blue eyes appraised the leader. "A female dog is still a bitch, different breed or no."

"The bear isn't his god, and he respects us for besting it."

"What else did he say?"

"That when one of their tribe has reached your age, they are usually content to sit beside the fire all day. He wonders if that is your normal position."

Rogan was not amused. "Inform this shaman that I could toss him into the fire and then warm myself in *that* glow."

"I'd better not, sire."

"Why does he hold the animal's entrails in his hands?"

After some discourse, Javan replied, "He uses them in a ceremony to divine the future."

Rogan's brow furrowed. "Wizardry no matter where I set my foot! Are there no peoples that simply hunt, drink, and fornicate? Wizards reading guts for fortune, even in un-known lands…"

The shaman's eyebrows narrowed. Javan frowned at Ro-gan and then spoke reassuringly to the shaman. Then he turned back to his uncle again.

"Sire," he said calmly, as if speaking to a child, "we are in their land. We should respect their ways."

Rogan eyed the group. "I could kill them all with no help from an archer. Why should I show them grace?"

"Uncle…"

Rogan shook his head in frustration. "So what has he seen, this shaman?"

Again, Javan translated, "He says that there is a great sadness where we come from."

"Bah! He's a huckster. How would he know where we come from, let alone the mood of its citizenry?"

Javan put both of his hands on his temples as he listened to the shaman talk.

"He claims the spirits told him through the entrails that the land where we come from is in chaos."

Rogan's patience vanished. His fingers played across the hilt of his broadsword. The natives stirred uneasily.

"Tell him to listen harder to those guts, root his snout among them like a swine, and tell me the name of our land—or he will hear what secrets his own guts have to tell with my blade buried in them."

"Sire," Javan exclaimed, his eyes wide. "Please?"

The two old men stepped to within inches of each other. The grim smile on the shaman's face matched Rogan's own. They stared into each other's eyes, and neither flinched or gave ground. A conversation seemed to be going on in their faces.

Rogan's softened first.

Javan gaped. He had seen Rogan break traitors to the kingdom and deserters from the army with a single stare. But now his uncle's will seemed to give under the unknown powers of this native, a man who had seen more winters than Rogan himself.

"What does he see, Javan? A cataclysm? A flood? I've heard the crazy prophets beyond the land of Shynar preach such an end is due the world; that we will all drown when Dagon's watery kingdom engulfs our lands, and the fledgling cult of the One true god near Ur floods us all. That eventually, we will all end up as floating bait for Leviathan and his ilk."

Javan considered admonishing his uncle for speaking aloud of one of the Thirteen, but then thought better of it.

"No, sire," he said. "He does not speak of a worldwide disaster. It is more personal. Albion is in tumult. The shaman says that dark men have overthrown the kingdom, and placed the sitting king in chains deep within the dungeons."

"Rohain?" Rogan asked, half-believing. "If that is so, then it is as the pirates testified."

"It appears so, sire," Javan said. "I fear for my cousins. And I—"

His voice trailed away.

"What is it, lad?"

"My father, sire."

"Thyssen? What of him?"

"The shaman has no news of him. Indeed, he cannot see him at all."

Rogan silently appraised the old man. Then he turned, placing one big hand on his nephew's shoulder.

"Javan, it is like my dream. I saw the evil of the world encroaching on Albion, like the wings of a bat. Rohain in chains—this was a fear of mine as well, but the vision was unclear."

Beyond the tree line, a great cat howled in the darkness. Rogan looked toward the forest, and the hairs on the back of his neck twitched. A feeling of uneasiness crept over him.

"By Wodan, Javan—they bring me such good news, these savages. Ask them if they are skilled at rowing a boat. Perhaps they can replace the Olmek-Tikalize."

The shaman spoke quickly. Javan hesitated.

Rogan raged at his inability to understand the conversation and barked, "What is he saying now?"

"They are aware of our plight, sire, and would like to help. But…"

"But what? What is it they seek? Gold? They suck at dry tits there."

"They are oppressed by an evil shaman named Amazarak, who dwells high up yonder mountain. This Amazarak serves a traveler—a strange being from afar. This traveler has enslaved many of their tribe, and is also the reason for the deformities that mar many of these folk."

Rogan studied the freakish appearance of a few of the red-skinned men. Now that they were illuminated fully by both the fire and moonlight, he could make out even more. Some had two noses or three eyes. Others were covered in boils or oozing sores. Many were completely hairless. One of them possessed a left eye that looked like a figure eight as it split into two orbs. And still another seemed to possess genitalia of extraordinary length and girth, if the bulge in his loincloth were any indication. Rogan had known concubines that would consider that last one a blessing rather than a curse.

Somewhere in the distance, a twig snapped. Again, the forest seemed to be alive, watching him, yet he could not see a thing.

"Oppressed by a wizard? Hah. Who isn't, these days? Why should we care?"

"Because he understood your words, sire, and sees that your son is in dire peril from his half-brother. The shaman calls his folk *Kennebeck*. He comprehends our plight that we are castaways here in the Kennebeck lands, and that we wish to leave."

"Then he's a powerful shaman." Rogan snorted, and looked at the foaming sea. "And he talks fast, too. He chatters like a monkey."

The old man kept talking and Javan interpreted. "There is a great tribal disagreement over what to do about this Amazarak. The Kennebeck have tried to fight him, yet they are powerless to defeat him. They hate to leave their sacred grounds of their kindred but are about to abandon them anyway."

"They flee?"

"They must escape, sire. To stay means enslavement or death. They have no choice but to leave. Yet they are loathe to abandon their imprisoned brothers."

"What does Amazarak want with slaves?"

"He does not. They are used by the one he serves, the one from afar. But the shaman knows not for what purpose. His visions do not show him, and no sentry has ever returned from the mountain."

"From hence does this foreign man come, this traveler? Near our home?"

Javan asked the shaman, and the old man pointed to the sky.

"The sky? So we fight more gods?" Rogan sheathed his weapon. "Does this dark traveler from the stars who is not a man have a name?"

Javan's eyes grew wide when he learned the answer. He was afraid to say the name out loud and refused to translate.

"Well?" Rogan shifted with impatience. "Whom do we fight?"

Javan whispered so quietly that Rogan had to strain to hear him.

"Croatoan."

The word hung in the still night air. Several of the Kennebeck tribe shivered.

"Never heard of him," Rogan frowned. "He must be from some paltry pantheon."

"Sire," Javan whispered, swallowing loudly. "Croatoan is another name for Meeble, who is one of the Thirteen, those who are not angel or demon, god or devil. Those who come from elsewhere."

After a deep breath, Rogan squeezed his eyes shut for a few moments. "I know who the Thirteen are, dammit. I saw you flinch when I mentioned Leviathan earlier. I know them well, and I don't fear them enough to memorize their names and sigils and houses." Rogan paused and muttered, "Meeble? Shit fire and save the flints." He cleared his throat and spoke louder. "What is our wolf-headed host's name?"

"This is Akibeel, sire."

Rogan shrugged and thrust out his hand. The shaman let the dripping intestines slip from his fingers and clasped it. The old man's slick, gnarled hands were warm and strong.

"Akibeel wishes for Amazarak to be destroyed and Croatoan to be sealed away from this world, before the tribe is all dead, and this great evil is loosed upon the rest of the land. Something terrible is brewing in the caves beneath the mountain's peak. Akibeel asks our help, for he sees experience with such matters in you, sire."

Rogan laughed. "Tell him that, as he has pointed out, I'm no longer a young man, and that I'm certainly no wizard. What can I do against this Croatoan, or Meeble, or whatever they wish to call him? The Thirteen may not be gods or devils, but they aren't mortal either. You know the legends as well as I do, Javan. I don't have the means to banish Croatoan from this level. I work with swords, axes, and pikes, and with my own two hands—not sigils, potions, and spells. Can the bastard bleed? If so, then perhaps we can talk."

"Akibeel does not know for sure, sire, but he believes that he may be able to provide a means if we can aid him. If Meeble gets loose in this world, he will go from community to community and destroy all."

Rogan started to reply, but then he grew distracted. He studied the restlessly milling natives, noticing their apparel.

"Why do they all wear necklaces of human fingers and ears?"

"Trophies, or totems as they call them, mementos of their conquered foes."

Akibeel was silent. He seemed to be waiting on Rogan's answer.

Rogan kicked the sand with his boot heel. "So, I must be a mercenary again, aye; a general for these Kennebeck? Perhaps I should've stayed in my bed in Albion after all and perished from oral oblations of the maids. That would have been a fine way to die; drained dry."

"Akibeel warns that if we do not help, there will be no world to go back to. Croatoan will move on to destroy more and more of the planet, until it is all gone."

"There isn't one man amongst his kin who will rise to the challenge?"

"He has some help, but not enough to attack Amazarak's black lodge."

"Is that his help that I smell in the woods?"

Javan translated for the shaman. Akibeel's smile faded and confusion clouded his face.

"I can smell the musk of a woman a mile off, Kennebeck man!" Rogan laughed. "Especially one in heat. Give me the wind and a stiff will and they are mine. A woman has never been able to hide from me, so why hide some in the forest?"

Akibeel understood Rogan's inference, if not his words. He muttered beneath his breath.

Javan said, "The women in the forest are not of his tribe, but aide his kin in their quest."

"Ask him why we should help him kill this shaman if he has a couple of women on his side? What do they need an old man and a boy for if he has a few tough women to hold his sack for him? Can he spirit me back to Albion if I do?"

"He promises to place enough men to man the boat at our disposal. They will help us repair it, thus to return home, if we aide his tribe. A few will also agree to serve as crew. And they will provide enough provisions to see us on our journey back across the sea."

"Or at least to our friends down south again. So they will fight behind me, but not for themselves? In my old age,

I am to serve as a mercenary general to an army, plying my skills the way the whores in Sodom do? By Wodan, what a damned joke! But if we wish to return home in time... Fine. I will accept the terms. But tell him if he leaves out any information or double crosses me, the next guts he reads will be his own."

Akibeel smiled, his black eyes signaling understanding.

Akibeel and his people slowly settled in around the campfire. Rogan eyed them uneasily, still not completely trusting their intentions. Javan, ever the diplomat, offered the Kennebecks fat slabs of cooked bear meat, which they gratefully accepted. They smacked their lips, rumbling with pleasure. One of the red-skinned natives produced a leather skin filled with liquor, and passed it around the circle. Rogan took a swig and handed it to Javan. The youth drank greedily, and then it made another round.

After a few draughts, the aged barbarian warmed up to his new employers.

"Tell Akibeel that his people make good wine."

Javan translated for Rogan. "He thanks you, sire, and promises there is more where that came from."

"Bring out these women," Rogan laughed. "I would see them. Why do they hide? Let them come forth and drink. Are they deformed like the men?"

The moon vanished behind dark clouds, and the campfire seemed to dim, as if swallowed by the darkness. Akibeel cried out in panic. He thrust a bony finger toward the distant mountain range.

Rogan yanked his sword from its sheath, half falling back on his ass. "What now, dammit?"

Javan said, "He fears that Amazarak is casting a spell from his lodge on high. They regret not bringing along their two champions to meet us."

"Champions?" Rogan grunted. "If they have these men, what need have they of us?"

"These two champions, Takala and Eyota, want no part of the fight. They wish to leave the area."

Akibeel grew more animated.

"He says the spell gets stronger. Be wary, sire."

Rogan eyed the shaman skeptically and then gazed at the dark mountaintop. "Akibeel can tell that from here, can he?"

"Apparently, sire."

The Kennebeck people quickly dispersed, fleeing towards the safety of the forest.

Rogan scowled. "Why do they run away?"

"They fear Amazarak's magic. Croatoan is hungry."

"Does he eat people?"

"I am not certain."

Akibeel gestured at the mountain. An emerald light now emanated from it.

"Wodan's sack," Rogan breathed. "Look at that! Sorcery if I've ever seen it."

"He says again to be cautious," Javan warned.

"For what?"

As if he'd understood the warrior king, Akibeel raised one trembling, gnarled finger and pointed at the ocean. Rogan and Javan turned, staring at the surf as something dark emerged from the water.

"Be wary of the dead." Javan gulped.

The clouds parted, and the moonlight revealed the true state of their enemy. A line of black corpses rose up from the waves. Saltwater dripped from their bloated flesh as they padded onto the sand. One of them still wore a necklace of tiger's teeth; the chain embedded in its swollen flesh. Another clutched a curved blade in its leathery fingers, yet in the top of his head gaped a hole. Seaweed and saltwater filled the space where his brain should have been. The creatures shambled toward them, their faint, soulless cries drifting across the beach.

Rogan recognized them immediately, despite their putrescence. These were the bodies of the corsairs they'd slain,

Karza's warriors, animated and seeking revenge, even beyond death.

"Zombies," Rogan muttered. "Wodan's balls, I hate zombies."

One's bloated stomach hung horribly swollen, as if it were pregnant with child. Another missed a leg below the knee. It hopped on one foot, collapsing every few yards. All of the corpses were in bad shape with shark-frayed ribbons of flesh hung from their frames. Broken bones poked through their mottled, parchment-thin skin, and shredded lips pulled back against shattered teeth. Their stench was horrific.

With a cry, a seagull darted down out of the night sky and pecked at one of the creature's ears, hoping to dislodge the morsel. The zombie reached up, grasped the bird in its fist, and squeezed. Then it flung the lifeless gull to the sand and continued approaching.

The sixth zombie to clamber across the beach was absent much of his skin, exposing muscles and veins. A sea-worm tunneled through its neck and another burrowed through its shoulder. One of the creature's eyes was missing, and a small hermit crab scuttled in the empty cavity. Seawater ran from the ghoul's gaping mouth. One of its arms was also gone. The hand on the other arm clutched a curved sword. The creature raised the weapon and pointed it at Rogan in recognition.

Sighing, Rogan turned his head, listening to his joints pop. "Is there no end to this madness? I have killed them once. Must I kill them a second time?"

Without waiting for a reply, he charged forward to meet his opponents, counting seven of the creatures on the beach, plus seven more heaving themselves from the water. He exploded into their midst, broadsword whistling through the air, cleaving rancid flesh, slicing through decaying muscle and tissue.

One of the zombies parried his follow-up attack, and their swords clanged together. Rogan turned his head away.

The stench wafting off the corpse made him gag. Blocking the curved blade's descent, Rogan grasped the undead warrior's arm and tried to pull him forward onto the point of his broadsword. Instead, the creature's skin slipped off, revealing bone. Rogan stared in horror as the thing *smiled*. Its face had been half-eaten by fish, and the fleshless cheek swarmed with larvae. A seashell jutted from the raw wound where its nose had been.

"Wodan take you, dead man," Rogan whispered.

The old king leaped into the air and lashed out with his leg, kicking the zombie in the head. His boot sank into the soft flesh. Rogan laughed as bits of brain matter and skull fragments splattered onto the wet sand. His landing, while graceful, was not nearly as nimble as it would have been ten years before. His agility, like the hair in his salt and pepper mane, lessened with the passing of each winter. Rogan spun on his heels, wheeling to face his next shuffling opponent.

Before he could renew his attack, several arrows sprouted from the chests and throats of the living dead. The shafts were not of the type Javan had been using. Rogan ducked, warned by some primal, battle-honed instinct, as more missiles flew from the forest. The arrows found homes in the monsters, but had no effect.

Several women stepped out of the shadowed woods, and silently reloaded their bows. Each sported flowing, shiny black hair; but none was of the Kennebeck tribe, nor of the ginger skinned Olmek-Tikalize from the southern continents. These tan women stood much taller, and their eyes were drawn up at the sides, almost like those from the distant Eastern lands that Rogan had raided as a teen.

"I grow weary of this," Rogan muttered, ducking the clumsy swing of a zombie. "Tonight, I merely wished to sit, drink and eat, and warm my bones beside the fire—and perhaps explore between the legs of one of these red-skinned or tan-skinned women, deformed or no. Now, instead, I slay those already dead."

The zombie's reply was a gurgled moan.

"To Hades with you all," Rogan roared and hacked the legs out from under it. "How many times must I kill your lot before you stay dead?"

The pathetic undead were not much of a fighting force. Still, they swarmed him with their numbers. More of the foul creatures poured from the sea. The female archers fell back, lest their hail of arrows strike Rogan. Pulling his sword, Javan sprang forth.

Rogan sliced another zombie in two at the belly. Undaunted, the corpse's lower half walked on. Its upper portion flopped into the water, and then pulled itself back across the sand. Rogan's sword fell once, twice, severing the arms. Then he cut the disembodied walking legs in half, dividing the hips. Something grasped his boot. He glanced down, shuddering in revulsion as the decaying hands trailed across his feet, dragging the severed arms behind them.

Javan brought down another slow moving corpse. A severed hand crawled up his back like a spider and clutched at his throat. Shuddering, he yanked the thing off and flung it into the ocean.

"Uncle," he shouted, "this is madness! There is no way to kill them. Each limb we hack off becomes yet another opponent."

"Tell that Kennebeck wizard that this is his kind of fight, not ours."

Javan confessed, "I can't."

"What do you mean you can't? Do as I say, boy."

"Akibeel isn't responding. He sits cross legged at the fire, ignoring my pleas. That is why I joined the battle late."

"What? The fool. He picks a poor time to rest!"

"I think he's in some sort of trance, sire."

Rogan spat onto the sand. "I hate wizards almost as much as I hate zombies."

The zombies encircled the two exhausted men. Javan and Rogan stood back-to-back, swords held ready. The undead moved closer. Javan winced at the stench. Rogan blinked sweat from his eyes. The corpses raised their weapons.

"WODANNNNNN!" Rogan roared, preparing himself for the onslaught.

Then, as abruptly as they'd emerged, the creatures fell limp and tottered into the surf.

Rogan prodded one of the corpses with his sword, but it did not move.

"This time, let us hope they stay dead."

"Indeed, sire."

The bodies began washing back out to sea with the next crashing wave.

Akibeel rose, opening his eyes and shouting into the heavens. Rogan followed his gaze, and noticed that the strange emerald light on the mountaintop had vanished as well.

Javan relayed, "Akibeel says that he placed himself in a spell and entreated his gods for a blessing. The blessing came."

"Well, Wodan bless my ass. How can I fight one such as that? No wonder his champions, Takala and Eyota, want to leave and won't even show up to face me. Will Amazarak summon the dead to accost us with every step we take towards his god? How do we know that this shaman didn't pull that trick to gain our compliance?"

Javan interpreted for Akibeel again and said, "He knows your doubts, but begs you not to worry."

Rogan eyed the strange women from the forest. "Why?"

"Because he will fight with you. He will stand by your *insides*."

"He will what? You have not translated correctly, boy. You meant to say that he will stand at my side."

Javan shook his head. "No, sire. Begging your pardon, but Akibeel distinctly said *insides*—I am sure of it."

The women drew closer. The tallest faced Rogan and spoke to him in a language he knew.

"We will fight beside you as well, if you will lead us. Do not discount Akibeel's powers, for they are great."

"Who the hell are you women?"

It was then that Rogan noticed all of them had only one breast. Their right breasts were missing. In their place stretched knotted scar tissue.

"I am Asenka," the tall woman said. "That name means *grace*. This is my sister, Zenata." She touched the shoulder of a younger female warrior. "Her name means *gift of God*."

"I am Rogan. That means *bloody bastard with a hard on*. This is Javan, which means *servant of a bloody bastard with a stiff cock*."

Javan stifled a grin.

Asenka's nostrils flared. "You will help us, oh man of Keltos?"

"First, how is it that you understand my speech, sister?" Rogan asked, sword inserted in the sand like a cane.

"We are all that remains of an ancient tribe that trekked across this land centuries ago. You have seen our skill with bows. That is why—"

"That's why your right tit is cut off," Rogan interrupted. "So you can shoot better. I've been around what there is of this world, and have seen the practice before, when I was a teen. Singed at birth or puberty, are you not?"

Asenka nodded in surprise.

"Well, at least you're on our side."

Asenka smiled. Her purple eyes nearly looked like coal.

Speaking in hurried whispers, Akibeel pawed at Javan's elbow.

Rogan frowned. "What is the old monkey chattering about now?"

"He says we should leave the beach now, before Amazarak sends more foes to test our strength."

Javan and Rogan agreed to let the thin red men of the forest gather up the weapons scavenged from the bireme, since they could not carry the load themselves. In quick order, they collected up the weapons, pieces of armor, and other useful items. The Kennebeck shaman summoned two-wheel wagons pulled by other tribesmen.

"First they call forth women warriors," Rogan said. "Now wagons. What else do they have hidden in yonder woods? Catapults? Perhaps a hundred fine horses?"

"Akibeel says that is all, sire."

Rogan stroked his graying beard. "Tell them to return and watch a few days after high tide. There are apt to be more weapons and armor drifting in on the bodies of the dead. Scavenge what they can. We will have need of it."

Javan and the women warriors followed the old shaman into the forest. Rogan looked back to the waves, caught his breath, and thought of his eldest son. Even now, Rohain, his flesh and blood whom he'd taught to hunt, fish, and kill, was probably in chains. And his survival, and the survival of their kingdom, depended on Rogan helping these strange folk slay their wizard and his evil pagan deity—one of the Thirteen themselves. Rogan felt something he had not experienced in many years.

Fear. Just a twinge, but there all the same.

Javan stopped at the tree line and looked back at his brooding uncle.

"Sire? We must be off. Is everything all right?"

Rogan frowned and looked to the sky.

"Just thinking, boy. Just thinking."

5 THE VILLAGE

DAWN ALMOST BROKE upon them by the time they drew near the village. The forest was lit with the gray-blue hues that exist just before the sunrise. The leaves swayed in the slight, cooling breeze. Birds sang out to one another from the treetops, squirrels ran along the branches, and a deer leaped across the trail in front of them, its antlers still covered with velvet. As they walked, the Kennebeck picked berries from bushes along the trail. Neither Rogan nor Javan had ever seen the fruit in their native lands and each eagerly tried one. Javan relished the flavor on his tongue. Rogan pronounced them not worth the effort, and instead, drained the last Kennebeck wineskin of its contents.

They walked single file along an old, rutted footpath. Akibeel took the lead and Rogan brought up the rear. A Kennebeck warrior lagged far behind, to guard their flank, while Zenata took point, running along ahead of the procession. The group moved silently, and even Javan remained quiet, his eyes drooping from weariness. Asenka walked between him and Rogan.

"How came you here, Rogan the bloody bastard with a stiff cock?" she asked.

"I was joking about the name."

"Oh?"

"Yeah, the bloody bastard part."

"What?"

"Never mind."

"How did you come to be here?"

Rogan yawned. "We took a wrong turn while heading to a famed Assyrian whorehouse and the gods dropped us here instead."

Asenka frowned. "You jest."

"Yes," Rogan nodded. "In truth, we were too weary from the whorehouse and could no longer pilot our vessel. So we made camp on yonder beach. Those whores will wear a man out."

Rogan's laughter boomed through the forest, sending a flock of birds screeching from their perches. A squirrel chattered angrily at him from the branches overhead. A barrage of nuts fell from the tree.

Asenka's voice dripped with sarcasm. "You still desire such action at your age?"

"I'm not dead yet." Rogan smirked, halting at the crest of a ridge that overlooked a lush valley. "Javan, tell this lass the story of Rogan's desire."

"Sire, you know it better than I."

"But I like to hear you tell it," Rogan insisted, cracking his knuckles.

Javan yawned and cleared his throat. "The bards sing a tune of how Rogan's father cut him from his mother's womb. The theory is that since Rogan never passed naturally from a female opening, he will go down to his death trying to replicate the experience in reverse."

"How droll." Asenka rolled her eyes.

Rogan shrugged. "It was a good line in the taverns of Luxor."

Some time passed before Asenka spoke again. She looked Rogan up and down, and her tone was tart. "So you are the legendary savage who made himself king? You are the man who carved his way to the throne of Albion and took the crown from Silex's head?"

"What if I am?"

"Are you not stunned that I know of you?"

Rogan's head began to throb, fatigue finally betraying him.

"I don't stun easily…" His voice faded.

"Sire?" Javan stepped closer.

Though his eyes were open, Rogan no longer beheld the forest. He reached out and grasped a tree branch for support. His breath came in short gasps, and his muscles trembled. His ears rang, and the strength vanished from his limbs.

Zenata had returned from her position at point, replaced by a Kennebeck warrior, and she joined her sister and Javan as they clustered around Rogan in concern.

"What ails the old one?" the young girl asked.

"We do not know," Asenka whispered. "He suddenly became as weak as a newborn foal."

Javan held on to Rogan's arm, so that he would not fall. "Lean on me, sire." Abruptly, Rogan stabilized. Pushing the youth aside, he stomped his feet and took a deep breath. "I'm fine, boy. But—Volstag is dead."

"What?"

"I can't explain it, Javan, but I saw it as if I were there. I beheld it as clearly as I'm seeing you. Volstag is gone."

"Who is this Volstag?" Asenka asked.

"General Volstag is Rogan's great uncle," Javan explained. "He advised Rogan's son, King Rohain, on matters of state."

"If he is this old one's great uncle," Asenka whispered in her sister's ear, "then he must be ancient."

Javan ignored them. "Sire, did you see a vision?"

"Pour the piss out of your ears, boy. Of course I had a vision. I saw this bastard son of mine, Karac, enter the war room of the palace, clear as if I was standing there. He was accompanied by dozens of black warriors. Rohain fought them mightily, as did your father Thyssen, but they were overcome. Karac slew Volstag. Impaled him on his sword and then opened him up from belly to neck. The bald bruiser is dead."

Rogan paused, letting the rage drain from him. When his emotions were under control once more, he continued. "That old prick taught me to fight with a dagger, and how to bring down a stag with my bare hands. And now he is dead. They cut his head off after his guts spilled out. His blood was all over the maps on the table."

Asenka folded her arms. "Are you touched in the head, old one?"

"Not so much that I can't cut your other tit off if you don't curb your damned tongue, woman."

Asenka bristled but Zenata held her back.

"Are you certain Volstag is dead, sire?" Javan asked.

"I saw it, Javan, just as clearly as I see you. They tossed his head amongst them like children at play. And Rohain is in chains. A prisoner of these swine!"

"What of my father?"

Rogan shook his mane. "I saw not his fate, boy. Thyssen slew many, but he was outnumbered. He jumped from the window of the tower when they surrounded him, but I saw naught after that. I fear the worst. How could he survive?"

Javan fell silent, his fists clenched at his sides. His mouth was a thin, tight line.

"Damn it all," Rogan grunted, "what afflicted me— more sorcery?"

The rest of the Kennebeck tribe had halted when they realized that Rogan and the others weren't with them. Now Akibeel stepped forward as the dawn's first light filtered down through the leafy canopy overhead. He spoke at length, making many hand gestures.

Sighing, Rogan moved away into the shadows of a broad oak tree. He pointedly ignored the shaman.

Javan translated, "Akibeel feels that you were sent a vision of your homeland."

"Akibeel feels his own limp manhood," Rogan murmured.

Zenata erupted with laughter at the jest. Asenka elbowed her in the ribs, still clearly offended with Rogan's barbaric reprimand.

"It is possible," Javan continued, "that some unknown power allows you to see these terrible things. Perhaps he is right."

"Why would some evil force grant me such a sight; to taunt me? No. The truth is more mundane. We cannot deny it. No need to make excuses for me, boy. Don't lie to an old liar. If I'm growing soft in the head, then so be it. It's not the death I would have chosen, but we have seen the effects of senility and it is useless to put up a fight."

"I do not think your wits are failing, sire. Perhaps it is the will of Wodan that you saw what is happening in Albion. He grants you a boon—strengthens your will to fight on. He grants me one, as well, if the vision of my own father's fate is correct."

Rogan dismissed the suggestion. "Horseshit. Wodan grants no boons. He sits on his mountain and shits out light upon the world. He gives us power at birth, and that's fucking all. What we make of life is just that. Wodan doesn't meddle in the affairs of humans, unlike other deities."

Asenka said, "He hardly seems like much of a god then."

"At least he doesn't require daily blood," Rogan replied, "or for his females to be mutilated at birth."

The warrior woman's hand unconsciously went to her missing breast. She opened her mouth to reply, but Rogan cut her off.

"Who would want to worship a god that constantly intervenes? I can wipe my own ass. I need no god to do it for me. Why do the dire demons of the Thirteen fuck with us all? They are acting like gods."

"I swear this," Javan said, squinting at the mention of the Thirteen, "if my father was truly slain, then I shall have revenge on Karac."

"We both will," Rogan grunted. "Keep that hate alive in your heart, lad. It'll warm you when nothing else will."

They continued on through the dense forest. Javan moved forward to speak more with Akibeel. Rogan scanned the lush foliage. Through the breaks in the trees, he caught an occasional glimpse of the distant mountain that towered over them. The mist around its peak hung tinged with a greenish hue.

"Javan," he called. "Attend me."

The youth trotted back to him. "Yes, sire?"

"That green mist that surrounds the mountain. What is it?"

Javan shrugged. "I assume this color is an effect of the sun and the mist, but I am not certain. Akibeel has not mentioned it."

Rogan drew him close and whispered, "You grow too complacent with that old shaman. Be on your guard."

"You do not trust him, Uncle? He reminds me of—"

"You alone do I trust, boy. I'll not hesitate to kill every damned one of them. Neither should you. Remember that. There's no room for sentiment in our task. Our only concern is doing what we must to get home."

Javan bowed slightly. "But of course, sire."

"I don't want to see you hesitate to kill these women, either. Only a weak man will be stopped from the death blow by emotion or deference to another gender."

"By your command."

Rogan sniffed the air. "I smell cook-fires. We must be nearing their village."

Sure enough, they rounded a curve and the Kennebeck village laid spread out before them; a series of well-made lodges nestled deep in the forest near the base of the mountain. The pyramid shaped dwellings were constructed from long branches wrapped in long canvasses and skins. Smoke trailed out of a few. A great cry went up amongst them as the rest of the tribe came out to greet them. Rogan studied the men. The tallest was six feet, but they were all slight of build.

"Quite a few of them," Rogan remarked. "I would think the members of the tribe were nearly all dead, judging by the tales Akibeel spun. But I see that it isn't so. They seem almost overpopulated."

"This village," Javan explained, "is but one in a chain of Kennebeck communities set about the base of these mountains. Akibeel says they stretch on and on in many rings. I doubt all of these folk are from this particular settlement."

"Look at them. They scurry like ants. I see brickwork, so they know masonry. Farming and agriculture are on display, as well. But they know not steel." He gestured toward a group of women working straight wooden staffs into spears or grafting flat stones onto axe handles.

Several women weaved between the returning party, carrying freshly baked bread cakes, armfuls of bedding, pitchers of water, and other containers. Their eyes widened when they beheld the two pale-skinned warriors. Rogan winked at them and then grabbed his crotch. The women looked away, giggling.

"What else did Akibeel tell you during our journey?" Rogan asked.

"Amazarak was a good man years ago, but was seduced into the dark ways by Croatoan. At one time, Amazarak was the elder shaman and Akibeel's teacher. But he grew restless in his old age and wanted more from life."

"Product of aging," Rogan grumbled. His nostrils flared. The scent of cooking food teased his senses. Without realizing it, he began to drool. "One thinks the eyes will be satisfied, but once they are, the heart aches for more. Once the heart is quelled, the body demands reassurance that it's still worthy of life. Once that is sated, the loins demand proof of life. Once that happens, the process repeats. After a long time, one asks, is there anything more?"

Javan blinked, taken aback by his king's confession of life. Rogan had never admitted to such things.

"Or so I read," Rogan snapped. "To Hades with all of that. Tell on, Javan."

Javan fought to hide his smile. "Well, Amazarak consulted with Croatoan and put himself in terrible agonies for power. Sire, you wouldn't believe what this man did to get close to his deity."

A red-skinned woman offered Rogan a tiny bowl full of ground meal. He took it and said, "I've traveled the world. The words like Shaman are only used for those who go through great sufferings for their gods. I wonder what this food is?"

Javan accepted a drink of water from another woman. "But Amazarak was not content with the powers bestowed upon him. He still seeks more."

"Is that why this tribe hasn't destroyed him?" Rogan asked, sniffing the bowl's contents. "Akibeel spoke of their tribe's champions; Takala and Eyote. Do they not have two balls enough between them to fight or organize a force?"

"Amazarak is high on the mountain and surrounds himself with warriors sporting weapons these folk cannot fight against."

Akibeel motioned for Rogan and Javan to sit. Asenka and Zenata joined them. Rogan sank onto a flattened stump and stretched his aching back. He dipped two fingers into the bowl and sampled the meal. Grunting his approval, Rogan ate. Javan was offered a bowl and did the same.

Two tall men of the Kennebeck tribe appeared from the forest. Unlike their fellow tribesmen, they were sturdily built. The deformities that plagued so many of the Kennebeck were absent from their own bodies. Unlike their pathetic brothers, these men looked battle-scarred, hearty, and well fed.

Immediately, Akibeel began admonishing with the two newcomers. Smug smiles appeared on their faces. They stared at Rogan and Javan.

"Javan," Rogan sighed wearily. "I grow tired of Akibeel's chatter. If you must tell me everything they say, perhaps we should just slay them all now and be done with it."

Zenata and Asenka glanced at each other, unsure if Rogan joked or not.

The two newcomers continued staring. One of them muttered something which caused gasps from the rest of the tribe. Their demeanor ran clearly disdainful of the new arrivals.

"Do those two wish to propose marriage to us?" Rogan asked. "If so, please explain to them that I was married once and have no plans to do so again."

"I do believe these are the champions, Takala and Eyota," Javan said. "They appear unimpressed with you and me, sire. Akibeel is angry because they refuse to treat us as welcomed guests. Takala just made a rude comment about your parentage."

Rogan's expression darkened. "What was it?"

"I do not know, sire," Javan lied. "My understanding of their language has failed me."

"I told you before, lad; don't lie to an old liar. Now, what did that ox say about my lineage?"

"I-I believe it may have involved a g-goat and perhaps a sheep herder."

Rogan stared at the two men as they argued with Akibeel, studying their voice tones and body language. The larger of the two champions shed his quiver of arrows, his belt, knife, and bow and stepped into the open of the clearing. Grinning, he pointed at Rogan.

"Apparently," Javan translated, "Takala intends to—"

"I know a challenge when I see one, Javan."

Javan eyed Eyota, only slightly shorter than Takala. Akibeel turned to Javan and spoke quickly.

"He says," Javan translated, "that I must fight the other after Takala kills you, sire."

"So be it." Rogan set his feet. He did not disarm, but neither did he draw steel. "This is a stupid waste of time, but I shall meet his challenge. This doesn't aid these people or get us home any faster. After I have slain him, I say we be done with this entire tribe and just kill them all."

Takala was almost as tall as Rogan, but the aged king outweighed him in mass and muscle. The two circled each other. Takala spat something in his dialect. Rogan remained silent. Takala said something else and several in the crowd laughed. Glowering, Rogan reached down, pulled his tunic aside, grasped his manhood, and waved it at the red-skinned warrior. The onlookers cheered.

Furious, Takala charged, fast and low, striking at Rogan's face with a curled fist. Rogan slapped the blow away. Both men circled each other like panthers. Takala jabbed at Rogan a few times, but the older man easily sidestepped each blow. His opponent was young, brash, and angry, and Rogan stepped light, content to wait. Takala scrambled forward, trying to grapple with Rogan. Gripping him around the waist, Rogan squeezed his kidneys. Grunting with pain, Takala slithered up, boxed Rogan's ears and slipped around behind the barbarian, never breaking the hold.

Asenka whispered to Javan, "It is silly that they fight. What a waste of life."

"Takala is insulted and his honor is at stake," Javan replied. "Eyota's, too. They refuse to ally themselves with us, and since we cannot join forces, they have decreed that two of us must die."

Asenka sniffed. "Men."

Twisting from side to side, Rogan grunted, attempting to kick the Kennebeck champion's groin. Takala dug his bare heels into the mud, trying to leverage himself enough to pull Rogan from his feet. The tendons on Rogan's sunburned forearms flexed as he seized the wrists around his waist. With fingers of iron, the old man dug into Takala's flesh and pressed down. Blood welled up around Rogan's fingertips as his fingernails dug deeper.

Takala screamed, but never abandoned his attack. Rogan's fingers were now slick with his blood. Takala dropped down, releasing Rogan, and threw his shoulder into the back of his opponent's legs. Unbalanced, Rogan tumbled onto his back.

The crowd cried out. Takala sprang to his feet and grabbed Rogan's ankles. He aimed a kick at Rogan's stomach, but then Rogan scissored his legs, tore them free of Takala's grip, and kicked the lean champion in the nose. Bones crunched beneath Rogan's boot heels and blood spurted from Takala's face. Cradling his nose, he stumbled away from the fight, crying out in pain.

"Enough," Rogan gasped, panting for breath. "It is time to end this. I'm still hungry and wish to continue with my meal."

Rogan climbed to his feet. Takala rushed him again. Rogan took a knee and struck upwards, snapping the champion's jaw with an uppercut. The crowd gasped at the sound. Again, Takala staggered away. Standing tall, Rogan swiftly stole across the grass and grappled with Takala, knocking him to the ground.

"You are no champion," Rogan taunted. "And you were not spawned from a man's seed. Instead, it's obvious that your father shat into your mother's womb."

Though the younger man could not understand Rogan's words, he understood their intent. Takala sprang from the ground and charged low. His shoulder slammed into the barbarian's abdomen. Grunting, Rogan moved back a few steps. Takala reached for Rogan's throat. Their hands met, all fingers interlocking. Knuckles popped. Rogan immediately brought all of his weight and force down on the smaller man. Even though he was pinned, Takala refused to yield. Takala's ruined teeth sought Rogan's ear, intent on ripping it off, but his mouth wouldn't work. Abruptly, he withdrew his face from the old man's mane. Rogan's hair fell away from his face. The crowd murmured, spying the same thing Takala had just learned.

Rogan's ear was missing already. In its place was only a mass of gnarled scar tissue.

"Someone beat you to it," Rogan growled. "And now I'll do to you what I did to them."

Roaring, Rogan snapped all the fingers on Takala's hands, and then went after his throat like a rabid hound. The Kennebeck warrior shrieked. Rogan's teeth sank into the soft flesh of Takala's neck. Twisting his head back and forth, Rogan yanked away, and spat a wad of bloody meat onto the ground. A fount of crimson spewed from the wound, spraying Rogan's face.

Rogan stood over Takala triumphantly as the dying man pawed at his throat with pathetic, broken fingers. Blood bubbles burst in the wound. Takala's legs twitched uncontrollably. Rogan prodded him with his foot and the man lay still. Takala's blood dripped from Rogan's chin and nose. The old warrior licked his lips and grinned.

Watching from the side, Asenka turned away.

"Your turn," Rogan said, slapping Javan on the back. "Make it quick. We are burning the day time."

Enraged, Eyota stepped into the clearing. He bowed his head over his fallen partner, then reached down, dipped his fingers in the blood, and painted crimson stripes across his nose, cheeks, and forehead. He beckoned to Javan.

Rogan snatched a skin from a passing Kennebeck woman and quenched his thirst. Then, without thinking, he smoothed his hair back over his mutilated ear.

Javan took off his quiver and handed it to Zenata. "Keep this safe for me?"

She gripped his arm. "Surely, you are no man-killer. You have the eyes and voice of a poet. You cannot hope to beat one so much larger than you!"

Javan dropped his bow and shrugged her off. "Just keep it safe. I shall be back for it momentarily."

"No more tarrying, Javan." Rogan returned to his bowl of ground meal, digging into it with bloody fingers. "End this distraction. Then you can ply this lass with your silver tongue."

Zenata blushed, and her sister frowned.

"You're a pig," Asenka said.

Rogan licked his fingers. "And do you ever lay with pigs? If so, come here and attend to me."

Gasping with disgust, Asenka looked away again.

Smiling, Javan walked into the clearing and nodded at his opponent.

Eyota beat his chest and grinned, setting his feet.

Rogan tossed the empty bowl aside and reached for a platter of fruit.

Javan calmly approached Eyota, dodged the first jab, and planted a boot in Eyota's groin. The brave doubled over, the air rushing from his lungs. Javan grabbed him by the hair and yanked him closer. Holding Eyota in a head-lock, Javan snapped the warrior's neck. Eyota sagged in Javan's arms. The youth dropped him like a sack of grain. Straightening his tunic, Javan winked at his uncle, and then smiled at Zenata.

Several in the crowd grumbled and hissed. One woman sobbed. But the majority cheered, pleased at the prowess the two newcomers had displayed. Surely, they whispered, the gods had sent these two pale-skinned warriors to help them best the wizard on the mountain and his dark god.

Javan crossed through the crowd.

"You took your time," Rogan mumbled around a mouthful of berries. Juice dribbled down his chin.

"I apologize, sire. I was distracted."

Rising to his feet again, Rogan walked over and grabbed Eyota's limp form. He laid the body on top of Takala's, so that their corpses formed a cross. Then, with a bellow, Rogan withdrew his sword and thrust it down like a spear, impaling both men.

"WOOODANNN!"

His shout echoed through the trees. Akibeel and the women warriors stared aghast. Leaving the sword in the two bodies, Rogan drew his dirk and knelt, using Takala's head as a pillow for his knee. Stabbing the dead man's hairless chest, Rogan split the ribs and cut out his heart.

Zenata cried out and averted her eyes. Several of the Kennebeck onlookers vomited or gagged. The rest gasped and murmured. But none of them dared to approach Rogan. Rogan stomped his foot at the crowd, and they fled for their huts and scattered into the forest. Overhead, a flock of shrieking birds soared into the sky.

"By the heavens," Asenka murmured, glancing around the deserted village, "they are all terrified of him now."

Javan nodded. "As well they should be. Did they think him an ancient and kindly patriarch of our far land, tired and worn?"

Laughing, Rogan took a huge bite from Takala's heart. Blood ran down his chin like plum juice. Swallowing, he then cast the organ aside.

"Is it bitter, Uncle?"

"Aye, Javan. Needs herbs."

As Rogan wrenched his sword free, Asenka coughed, suppressing her gag reflex.

"That was barbaric!"

Javan seemed surprised. "He is a barbarian, miss. Did you think otherwise?"

"But he is a king—a ruler."

"And a good one," Javan confirmed. "But he is not as sophisticated as those he ruled. He is unlike anyone else to ever sit on Albion's throne. You and your sister indicated before that you knew the stories of how he gained the throne. Did those methods seem civilized to you?"

"No. But this…"

Drawing his own dirk, Javan then walked over to the body of Eyota. Zenata followed him, curious. Cutting through the man's loincloth, Javan stabbed upward and sliced quickly. Then he deposited his extracted prize on Eyota's head.

Zenata grabbed Javan by the elbow and turned him around. "You say that your uncle is a barbarian, but then you cut off Eyota's balls and place them on his face? You call that proper and civilized?"

Javan spoke somberly. "I do indeed. Most cultures believe the eyes are the windows to the soul, as do these people, if I've correctly understood everything Akibeel has told me. The first things the ravens will eat are Eyota's eyes, so I covered them, giving his soul a fighting chance to leave first, should it choose to tarry in the confusion following his sudden death."

Zenata was speechless.

"Come." Rogan wiped his sword in Zenata's hair, causing her to scream and run. "I have asked Wodan for his blessing on this venture with the blood of these fools. If he chooses not to recognize it, piss on him. We have more pressing matters, and I would sample more of the Kennebeck's liquor, and perhaps one or both of these one-breasted women."

Asenka bristled. She opened her mouth to retort, but Rogan cut her off with a grin. Arm outstretched, he motioned with his hand.

"If that is a yes, then shall we retire into the lodge?"

In his years of travel and adventure, Rogan had heard women curse in many languages.

None of them compared to Asenka's.

6 PRINCE OF THE EARTH

AKIBEEL'S LODGE, WHILE similarly pyramidal, towered much larger than the other dwellings in the village. He ushered Rogan, Javan, Asenka, and Zenata inside. Accompanying them were two more of Asenka's warrior women. Both of them eyed Rogan suspiciously. Also on hand were two of Akibeel's mutant tribe mates; both male, one with a cleft palate and the other with an oversized singular eye in the middle of his face. Female attendants bustled in, carrying bowls and platters heaped with food. Each of the women also had noticeable birth defects.

The interior of the lodge was warm and dry. Sweet smelling smoke drifted from incense-filled earthen bowls; their sides painted with mystic symbols. Animal skins, sprigs of plants, and various totems lay scattered about, all for use by the shaman in his pagan ceremonies.

Rogan took a drink of cold, clear spring water and swilled it about in his mouth. He noticed that Zenata watched Javan closely.

"Careful, Javan," he whispered in their own tongue, so that the others would not hear. "The young one eyes you like you were sweet candy."

Javan gnawed a chicken leg. "Only an ignorant man wouldn't note the desire of a lass."

"What fool philosopher are you quoting now?"

"You, sire."

"Nonsense," Rogan grunted. "If that's true, then I must have been drunk when I said it."

"Quite probable, sire. Still, I knew the possibilities of paradise as well as the pitfalls of failure when I set out on this journey with you."

Rogan chuckled. "You talk too much, boy."

Though the Kennebeck folk had fallen on hard times, they managed to present a meal befitting the two newcomers. There was fire-roasted chicken stuffed with herbs; venison and rabbit; a thick, savory fish stew; flat cornbread, still warm from the hearth and slathered with rich, creamy butter; and nuts, fruits, and vegetables aplenty. They washed it down with water and wine, both of which flowed freely.

Rogan grunted in appreciation, wiping his mouth with the back of his hand. "Tell Akibeel I have not had venison this good since my time in Shynar."

Javan passed the message along. The old shaman smiled and bowed graciously. Then his face grew grave again. He chewed half-heartedly at a crust of bread. Rogan noticed that Akibeel's eyes lingered on his deformed attendants.

Rogan studied the servant with the cleft palate and his cyclopean companion. "So these hideous defects, they are caused by Amazarak's magic?"

Javan nodded. "They are infected with Croatoan's green light. Apparently, the green light springs forth from some sort of otherworldly device. And Akibeel says that an even worse price can be exacted."

"This price seems grave. What price could be worse?"

"The loss of their souls, sire. They say Amazarak is a soul collector for Croatoan. Once his work with their bodies is through, he steals their souls. His black lodge on the mountain is the abode of these souls."

"Does he take their kin regularly?" Rogan accepted a bunch of green grapes from an attendant, and popped some into his mouth.

Javan nodded. "Amazarak's loyalists steal away the children and full grown females and use them for sacrifice. He has a great force of former Kennebeck tribesmen at his disposal. They obey Amazarak's orders because he controls their souls. Akibeel says that many suspected Takala and Eyota of being in league with Amazarak."

"Not any longer."

"True, Uncle."

"Why don't Akibeel's people rise up and fight?"

"They try to, sire. But Amazarak's raiders are armed with steel, and as you noted earlier, these people are not."

"So they want us to kill this Amazarak. If he has warriors with steel, we are but two men."

Asenka frowned. "What of us, old man? I can stop the life of anyone, wizard or warrior."

"I stand corrected," Rogan said. "We are but two men and a couple of female distractions. Once we destroy Amazarak's forces, what then? How can I fight him or Croatoan? I am no wizard. I care little to dance with a devil at this stage in my life, or any other. I have done enough of that in the past."

Akibeel patted Rogan on both shoulders and spoke to Javan.

"He says leave Amazarak to him," Javan translated. "He will fight inside you."

Rogan frowned. "That is the second time he's said that. I like not the sound of it."

Akibeel spoke quickly. His spirits seemed to be lifting now that Rogan was expressing an interest.

Javan continued. "He says that your body and spirit are what he needs. Both are strong enough to best his rival. Akibeel thinks that his gods have sent you to destroy the devil on the mountain, as well. He sees it in his prophecies. A stranger not of this land is the only one to upset the balance of evil."

"I love the sound of that." Rogan's tone dripped with sarcasm. "Javan, I don't trust these men, but what can we do?"

"We could just start a long journey overland, sire, and hope we go far enough south to find our friends in Ol-mek-Tikal."

"That crossed my thoughts, but it would take ages and I think our time is at a limit. We are needed across the ocean. Every day we remain here could cost them their lives."

"Yes, sire, my thoughts truly."

"Go back to your fallen kingdom," Asenka said. "They do not need your sword. We will stay and aid them. The Kennebeck have fed us, made us welcome in their home. We shall stand by them."

"You?" Rogan laughed. "That is a fine jest—a band of one-breasted women against this steel-wielding army."

Asenka glared at him, her purple eyes unblinking. "We are not afraid, old man. Can you say the same?"

Rogan sprang to his feet, knocking aside a platter of nuts. "By Wodan, no woman speaks to me such. Arise, bitch, so that I may knock you down. It occurs to me that your mouth needs something to keep it busy."

All four of the warrior women immediately jumped to their feet and drew their weapons. Akibeel let out a startled squawk, and the attendants shrank away, dropping platters and pitchers. Javan quickly moved between Rogan and Asenka, his arms outstretched, palms up.

"Please," he said. "Need I remind you all that we are guests in this lodge?"

"Still your tongue, boy," Rogan growled. "Or I'll deal with you next."

"While you're doling out punishment," Asenka spat, "you could instead focus your rage on these people's oppressors."

"Oh? Tell me, woman, how are we to fight all of Ama-zarak's hordes? There will be far more than the dozen dead men who assailed us on the beach."

"The Kennebeck don't know how to forge steel, old man, but you do. You can teach them."

Rogan raised an eyebrow, and turned to Javan. "Have you not wondered how this Amazarak knows the secret of steel, but these people do not? Aren't they both originally from the same tribe?"

Javan translated for Akibeel. "Amazarak tapped an entity from beyond to work in steel even before the arrival of Croatoan, a creature called Azazyel. He gave the wizard the secret of steel in exchange for—"

Rogan sat again, his anger at the women forgotten, and waved a huge hand. "Yes, yes, all of these gods and devils want blood and children. I've heard that song before and never had understood the tune. Wodan be praised for his disregard of this world. At least he isn't a vampire screaming for the blood of infants."

"There is another obstacle as well, sire, but I'm not sure that I can translate it properly. I believe he's saying 'giants', but I'm not sure."

"Giants? I have slain several in my time."

Akibeel chattered with irritation. Javan suppressed a laugh.

"What is he saying?" Rogan asked.

"It seems that Akibeel grows as frustrated with the pace of my translations as you do, sire. He wishes to consult with forces beyond so that he can speak to you directly. He asks that we give him a few moments to prepare, and invites us all to continue with our meals."

They all sat again. The warrior women moved away from Rogan and Javan, shooting them wary glances as they ate.

"Sire," Javan whispered, "tell me again of your vision."

Rogan took a bite of corn. "There was something wrong, Javan. Truly, the palace was deceived. We must have been betrayed from within."

"Why do you think that, sire?"

"The slaves, surely servants of this Karac, were allowed in close. So there was treachery from within. But this Karac, the one that is to have been my son, he sported long locks of shaggy hair."

Javan gnawed at a rabbit leg. "And why does that trouble you?"

Rogan frowned. "Because they shear down slaves so that lice cannot spread. No matter if they work in the field or as teamsters. The other blacks in the palace were bald, but Karac had hair."

"Fascinating."

"I can see the damned teamsters arguing with Volstag, wanting more pay and inserting a newcomer like that to make him angry. But never mind that. We were betrayed, plain and simple. And perhaps not just by our slaves. There were maps on the table, Javan. Maps of other lands—as if they were preparing for war."

"Surely the neighboring lands are your allies, friends of yours!"

Rogan nodded. "But they may fear me and not Rohain. They want to test his sack and how effectively he can use it. The fact that he may have an heir in his wife's belly is no sign of achievement. Dogs have workable cocks, Javan."

"True enough, sire." Javan saw Zenata suppress a grin.

Akibeel returned with a small clay bowl, filled with dry sage. He placed the bowl on the floor and produced a flint. Soon, thin lines of grey smoke drifted from the burning sage. Akibeel left again.

Rogan patted the ground next to him and nodded at Zenata and Asenka. "No sense sitting over there. If you intend to join forces with this old man and his nephew, then join us. Bring your warriors, too. It will not be the first time I have lain with more than one woman at the same time."

Asenka said, "Never dream of trying to lay down with me, old fool."

Rogan chuckled. "I'd sooner lay down with a demon. It would be hotter, no?"

Javan offered Zenata a spot beside him. "Certainly not the first time that event would have happened, aye sire?"

Akibeel returned again and stripped off his garments, standing naked before his guests. The lodge filled with smoke. The servants lowered rawhide straps from the ceiling. The straps had sharp bones on the end of them. Rogan and Javan watched in silence as servants inserted these bony spikes under the muscle and tendons in Akibeel's pectoral area. Another servant used a stone knife to make several small cuts on the shaman's back. More of the thongs were then inserted into the wounds. Akibeel did not make a sound through the entire process.

"He can take pain, at least," Rogan said with admiration. "I am impressed."

Slowly, Akibeel was raised from the ground. He moaned as the thongs pulled tight, and screamed in agony as his chest pointed up to the ceiling. Drumming began outside the lodge, surrounding them. Rogan panicked, believing the drums to be a signal of attack, but the servants made no move towards him. They simply held the straps taut, chanting with a low and monotonous rhythm. Akibeel screamed again. Then, the mutant with the single eye drew near to Rogan and Javan. Asenka and Zenata jumped up, their hands on their weapons. The one-eyed apprentice came closer. Rogan could smell his sour breath. The deformed servant grinned; a long thread of drool hung from his bottom lip.

Cursing, Rogan drew his sword.

"Put it away, barbarian."

The deep voice belonged to Akibeel. Rogan was shocked to learn that he could now understand him. But his voice—his tone—had changed. It was guttural. Unnatural. Booming. The silver hairs on Rogan's arms stood up.

Javan knew that it wasn't the shaman who spoke. It was something else, using his voice. He addressed Akibeel's suspended form. "Who are you?"

Akibeel glanced over his shoulder. His face was drenched in sweat. His eyes were pure white. The pupils had rolled back in his skull. A glow rippled over his body.

"I speak through this man to encourage you to ascend to the top of the mountain."

"And who are you that I should be so honored?" Rogan sneered, hand still on his sword. "You're not Akibeel. That much is certain. Am I a dog that I should go piss when you say so? What is your name?"

"Names have power, barbarian, and I have many of them. I am one of those who observes the Earth and guards it. You may call me the Doorkeeper."

"Yes," Rogan grumbled. "And I bear the mark of Cain on my ass!"

"Do not mock me."

Rogan persisted. "You say that you guard the Earth. If that is so, then why have you let this evil thing loose on the world? You do a piss poor duty, I must say."

Blood dripped from Akibeel's wounds. The straps pulled taut.

"My kind let nothing free. Your kind called on the murky depths and they answered with eldritch force. We are not God nor can we be everywhere in the cosmos at once. Look here at what is happening."

The flesh of the shaman's stomach glowed orange and then became transparent. They could see the twisted guts inside. Then, his intestines and other organs vanished. A swirl of images appeared. Everyone in the lodge grew dizzy as they watched, yet they could not tear their gaze away. The vision was like a moving picture, showing many primitive, subhuman ape-like men with reddish fur covering their bodies. They flowed from the mouth of a cavern in a glacial mountainside.

"I've heard of such creatures in the ancient of days," Rogan murmured. "This is madness for us to be seeing such a thing."

"Look," cried Zenata, squeezing Javan's arm. "There is Amazarak's lodge."

The scene now showed a pyramidal shaped building. It looked much like the one they currently stood in, but it was larger and solid black. Dimly, they saw a group of Kenne-beck slaves behind the lodge. Each man's skin was covered in horrid blisters and they were hideously deformed—much worse than the folk in the village. Then the image blurred.

Javan shivered. "Listen. Do the rest of you hear it?"

From Akibeel's belly came the sound of supplication. Another scene appeared. Amazarak stood at the mouth of another series of caves. He looked enough like Akibeel to be his brother, Javan thought. He even wore a wolfish headdress. Out of the caves bounded more of the red-furred creatures. They ravaged female captives staked out spread eagle for them. Javan wondered how any of the women survived such copulations. To be impregnated in such an unspeakable manner was too horrifying to think about. The image then changed again.

"I do not understand," Rogan muttered.

"Nor do I," Asenka agreed. "What is the meaning of all this?"

"I believe the vision is moving forward in time," Javan explained. "Look there."

They saw that none of the women had survived the childbirth process. They then saw an image of the monstrous offspring fully grown. Then the vision faded, and the shaman's stomach was flesh again.

Akibeel said, "This is the product of Amazarak's wickedness."

Rogan and the others realized that Akibeel was speaking with his own voice, yet they could understand him as if he were still possessed. Whomever—whatever—the Door-keeper had been, its presence had now departed, but it had left this gift of translation behind.

"Wizardry," Rogan said, spitting on the lodge's floor.

"Perhaps," Javan said, "but it will make things easier, sire."

Akibeel sounded like he was in great pain as he continued. "This race of giants is seen whenever we try to ascend the mountains. My people cannot fight ones such as them."

"How many are there?"

"Dozens. They are spread out and act as sentries. Our men fear them, so it is pointless to go. A man of steel could slay them."

"So in addition to his magic and his demonic cohort and his army of soulless Kennebeck men, Amazarak also has these half-human, half-ape offspring? And if I slay these beasts and defeat Croatoan and kill that blasted wizard and everything else that dwells upon the mountain, you will repair and man my boat and get Javan and I home?"

Despite his agony, Akibeel smiled and nodded. His servants lowered him down and removed the barbs from his flesh. Then they coated the wounds with salve and bound them.

Rogan scratched his head. "There's one thing I still don't understand. Why doesn't this wizard or Croatoan just destroy you all and be done with it?"

Akibeel sipped cold water from a clay mug. "It seems that we haven't yet finished whatever dark purpose he has planned for us. I fear there is a worse evil than this brewing above."

"With the turmoil in my homeland," Rogan said, "I think we have little time. Forging new weapons for your tribe would take too long, as would teaching you the ways of iron and steel. However, I can perhaps use the pieces we have to our advantage."

"How?"

Rogan turned to his nephew. "Javan, gather all the swords and lances we rescued from the shipwreck. These natives seem keen on using arrows. By Wodan, I will give them arrowheads that will slay the Dark One himself."

"Right away, sire."

Akibeel ordered two of the braves to help the young man.

Rogan stepped outside the lodge and took a breath. He then looked down at the ring of Kennebeck folk, sitting with small drums on their laps. No longer afraid of him, they smiled at the aging barbarian with snaggle-toothed grins. Javan, Asenka, Zenata, and the others exited the lodge behind him.

"Why the drums?" Rogan asked Akibeel as he emerged, limping. "In the jungles, the natives use them to communicate or summon their gods. Is it the same here?"

Akibeel steadied himself with the help of a servant. "These drums channel great medicine, King Rogan. Their covers are fashioned from the stomach skin of our enemies."

The old barbarian chuckled. "Do you know what I do with the stomachs of my enemies?"

Akibeel shook his head. "No. What do you do with their stomachs?"

"On the battlefield, I slice them open and crouch over-top them. Then I shit into the wound."

Asenka mumbled, "And he dares to call these people primitive."

If Rogan heard her, he gave no indication. Instead, his eyes turned upward once more, searching the sky through the high tree tops.

Javan noticed and wondered what he was looking for.

"Do we have time for sleep?" Rogan laughed. "I need some." He kept giggling, saying low, "Like I have time to shit after a battle."

Two days after they came to dwell amongst the Kennebeck folk, Rogan dreamt of more horrors. His frenzied cries awoke Javan. Javan rushed to his uncle's side. Covered in sweat, Rogan's eyes burned dangerous. His fists clenched his bedding.

"What was the dream, my Lord?"

Panting, Rogan waved a hand. "Get out of my sight, damn you. Leave me be!"

Accustomed to his master's rages, Javan opened the flap, glanced back at Rogan, and walked out into the night.

Sighing, Rogan lay back on the straw mat. Though he regretted imparting his anger on the youngster, he did not want Javan to see how weak and scared he felt.

"Hopeless and helpless," he muttered. "It's a wonder I've had any sleep at all this night."

There was a rustling sound from outside the tent. Rogan's head jerked to the left. His nostrils flared, registering a scent. He grunted and coughed, and then breathed low and shallow, pretending to go back to sleep.

Asenka leapt through the flap and charged him. She shrieked when she saw that Rogan's eyes were open. Before she could react, he jumped up and grabbed her wrists. Flinging her down on her back, he pinned her to the mattress. Squealing, Asenka slithered under his grip, but could not throw him off her. To avoid her kicks, Rogan pinned her calves down with his.

"You desire me so much, Asenka?"

She twisted and bucked, pushing him upward.

Releasing her, Rogan stood up. He grinned in the darkness.

"You think you bested me?" Asenka asked. "If I'd come to kill, you would already be dead."

"If you came to kill me, you would have worn clothes."

Asenka hooked her foot through Rogan's leg. With a quick maneuver, she knocked him off his balance. Rogan landed on his back, the air rushing from his lungs. Asenka jumped up and straddled him. She slapped his face, and then reached down to grab his manhood.

"I take what I want, old man." Her hand made a fist and pulled on his member. "Indeed, are you still a man after all these years?"

"I am," he said, as his manhood stirred, "when need be."

Rogan stiffened in her hand, and Asenka's eyes widened. When he started to sit up, she struck him across the face again with her other hand. Grinning, the old king lay back.

Asenka brought the head of his organ to her clitoris. Repeatedly, she ground him against her in small, circular motions.

Rogan did not object. He lay there in contentment, watching.

The woman worked up a slight sweat, grunting deep in her throat. Throwing back her dark hair, she stifled a moan. Her one lone nipple grew hard and Rogan reached for it, but she batted his hand away. Asenka began to tremble. Her breathing quickened. Unable to maintain her silence, she cried out and fell atop Rogan.

"As you can see," Rogan whispered, "I am still capable of pleasing a woman."

Her nails dug into his collarbones. "Don't flatter yourself, barbarian."

"Really? Then how about…"

Asenka's eyes widened as she felt his turgid member slap her buttocks. He clutched her hips with his strong hands. Biting her bottom lip, she pushed her pelvis back, slowly letting him enter her. Gritting her teeth, Asenka worked her hips back, slowly taking him in.

With a scream, she slammed herself down on him. She did not care who heard them. Tearing into his chest, she slapped and beat on him as they moved together. Rogan took the punishment and stayed on his back.

After a long time, Asenka trembled and howled again. She coasted to a stop and then leapt off him. She turned, meaning to run out of the tent, but Rogan swiped his feet together, tripping her. She fell half out of the tent. Rogan grabbed her ankles and dragged her back in. Again, he pinned her down, this time on her belly.

"Enough of me being the bitch," Rogan muttered in Asenka's ear, entering her from behind.

He thrust against her and soon joined her in her howls. Sated, he then lay back down and sighed. Asenka stood up, staggered, and then knelt beside him. She lay on his left side, her one breast lying on his chest. Rogan did not hold her or speak. He merely stared at the top of the tent.

"I am curious," she said, breaking the silence.

Rogan groaned. "Asenka, please don't ask me how I feel or demand that I make promises."

Again, her nails dug into his chest. "I was going to ask about your vision."

Rogan frowned. "I'd rather talk about your antics on the mat. I was impressed. I'm sure the others heard our passion."

"I don't care if they did. Your vision…"

"What of it?"

"What did you see?"

"I saw great peril in my former kingdom. This was bound to happen sooner or later. I overthrew the sitting king long ago and the world is a bad place. It's not a wonder such a thing came to pass. But I thought that my son and his advisors—men I've fought and bled with—would be able to meet any such action. I was wrong. Bloody days never seemed to end in the vision. The people I freed from the yoke of an evil king are now subjugated to greater horrors. Their daughters are forced to copulate with the invaders to create a new generation while their fathers and brothers are methodically slain."

"Such savagery," she replied.

Rogan looked down at her leg nestled over his body. "Surely, in your homeland there were wars and kingdoms overthrown?"

"Certainly; most tribal leaders fight their entire lives. Civilized kingdoms often fall from within. I have heard of some societies that collapsed and their remnants forgot everything learned in a generation."

"Perhaps," Rogan snorted. "But mankind will always find a way. If the world was burned to a cinder or flooded to the highest mountaintop, as the soothsayers believe it will be one day, and there were but a dozen people left alive, the wheel and the craft of steel would be found again. Life is a circle, girl."

"Do not refer to me as girl, barbarian. I am a woman."

Rogan took a breath. "I'd say so. My apologies."

Asenka smiled, hand tussling his long hair. "So you feel for your countrymen, especially the womenfolk?"

"No. They only have themselves to blame."

"What?"

Rogan nodded. "They could always die, couldn't they? Commit suicide rather than copulate unwillingly? Or kill themselves while their oppressors' seed grows inside them."

"But…" Asenka struggled for words. "You mean you'd see them willingly die just so they can't give birth to more of their subjugators?"

He stroked her hair. "Let that be a lesson to you. I'd kill myself to see this Karac dead."

"That is terrible, thinking so little of your subjects."

"They are good folks indeed, woman. However, my anger, my…feeling is harder for my own blood kin. That's how it should be. Growing up, I never had family save for my father. That's how it ought to be. You are unencumbered by sentiment that way. Then again, if my father hadn't desired to raise me as a warrior, he wouldn't have cut me from my mother's belly and stole me from her people."

Asenka shook her head in disbelief. "So it is weak to desire companionship? To want a partner to share life with? You think it is bad to desire love?"

Rogan blinked. "You place words in my mouth, woman. I grew up a fighter, a rover, a soldier, seeing wealth and warmth and never having it. The eyes are keys to the gut, and my guts were often empty. The rich had food and jewels to buy all that they needed, including a new woman. Why would love enter into it?"

"You are a savage."

Rogan was unapologetic. "And your point is? I wanted to be a ruler, a king, to have what I always desired—ultimate power. Once I took the crown of Albion, even more fighting went on. There was always a bastard around to try to take my crown. On a tower of skulls, I built my throne and knew peace at last."

"And yet, you are here."

Rogan was silent for a long time and then said, "I was bored, so I left."

"I disagree that you knew no love. Truly, love makes one strong."

"No, it doesn't. Love makes you do stupid things. It makes you create images of yourself. It lets you hold a tiny hand in your own. It makes you feel and desire odd things like seeing grandchildren. It gives you a weakness."

"You miss your queen?"

"I can buy another wife, but not another son or daughter. You see, that's what love does to you. It makes you care. Since my son and my family are in peril, I'd do anything to stop those attacking them. Karac knew it. My enemies have used that weakness against me. They have exploited it. A strong man would sail off and pass wind in the direction of Albion. Me? I am weak, for I would bite the balls off Satan himself to get at the ones who harm my children. That's what love brings—a chink in the armor."

"Did you love your queen?"

Rogan slipped out from beneath her and stood up. Stretching, he looked out of the tent flap.

"You make me talk too much, woman."

"How did she die?"

"A child killed her," Rogan said. "She had a baby and never recovered."

"I am sorry…"

Rogan tensed. "Get out of here and leave me be. You got what you came for. More actually. Go."

Donning her clothes, Asenka exited the tent and left Rogan to his brooding. A campfire glowed at the edge of the village. As she approached it, she saw Javan and Zenata sitting close together, the glowing embers flickering off their faces. They said nothing as she approached, but both of them smiled. Asenka sat down and looked into the fire.

"Save your smiles," Asenka snapped. "I do not love your master, Javan."

"I would never presume that you did, miss. In truth, it is just as well that you don't love him."

"Why?"

"Because eventually, everyone that loves Rogan dies…"

"You have known him your entire life, no? You don't love him?"

Javan stoked the fire. "No, I don't love him. He is not a man that easily allows that. I respect him, admire him, and would certainly give my life for him—and indeed, I probably will end up dying for him before we leave this land—but nay, there is no love there. I cannot allow myself that weakness."

"You are a strange pair." Asenka noted how close Zenata sat to Javan and how she looked at him when he wasn't aware. "Did Rogan love his queen?"

Javan raised an eyebrow. "All this talk of love is unseemly and strange to my ears. I am not a bard. But since you asked about the queen, I was a young man when she passed, but I do recall her. She died after her last child, a daughter. Did my uncle love her? Well, their relationship was more like fencing, to be frank. I think she loved Rogan. Very much so."

Asenka persisted, "But did he love her?"

"As often as he could, in his fashion. And she seemed satisfied with that. But Rogan does love his children unto death. That much is certain."

"How can he love his own children so much, but not feel the same for their mother?"

"Because it is easier to love those of your own blood rather than just a partner. That is the way of the barbarian— and my uncle is a barbarian before anything else."

"What say you? Are your thoughts the same in regards to love?"

"I am from Albion," Javan said, smiling. "Though

probably coarse in your eyes, we have a more advanced way of being. I have known the love of a partner, and hope to know it again."

Javan's eyes went to Zenata and then looked quickly away. Both blushed.

Asenka stood. "Rogan told me of his vision. He never shared that with you, his faithful servant. I know. I was outside the tent when you left."

Javan shrugged. "He is teaching me the ways of life, miss. I am not his slave. I am his nephew and loyal subject. Besides, he will tell me in time."

"Ha! Why do you think so?"

Javan's smile faded and he stared into the fire. There was a deep sadness about him.

"Tell me," Asenka demanded. "Why will he share it with you if he is so incapable of love?"

"Because," Javan whispered, his eyes not leaving the flickering flames. "I am all he has left, and we are a long way from home."

7 SIZE MATTERS

DURING THE NEXT few days, Rogan and Javan took the longer steel weapons salvaged from the wreckage of the ship and worked them into smaller implements—daggers, arrowheads, spearheads, and axe heads, since the tribe was skilled at using those weapons. There was no time to teach the Kennebeck of swordplay. Besides, an axe or spear in their hands could be just as deadly. Rogan was glad to perform the work. It took his mind off the events transpiring across the sea. While they manufactured the weapons, Asenka and Zenata trained the men of the tribe on better methods of fighting.

The sun rose high into the sky. The village buzzed with activity. Rogan and Javan labored with the weapons, while Akibeel sat nearby, head bowed in prayer. Asenka and Zenata had gathered their women warriors and the Kennebecks in a large clearing. The rest of the tribe busied themselves with preparation.

Rogan sweated over the fire, beating an arrowhead into shape with a stone hammer trimmed with metal. He swatted with irritation at a mosquito and then surveyed his handiwork.

"These weapons will make for a great equalizer. Amazarak's forces will be stunned when they have to face the Kennebeck folk armed with steel. And the loyalty we glean from these people will be a good thing later."

"True enough, sire," Javan answered.

His voice sounded far away. Rogan noticed that Javan studied Zenata, who taught hand-to-hand combat in the clearing. They watched as Zenata flipped her pupil over her shoulder for the third time. The other tribesmen laughed.

"I think the women are training dogs to shave. A hopeless task, I reckon."

"And still, they try," Javan murmured, his usual stoic manner dreamy as he watched. "They are noble savages. They have heart, if not the skills. And that may win the day. They will be ready."

"They had better be. Time draws short." He glanced down at the weapons. "But we have stacked more weight on the scale, eh? And they seem proficient enough with these. Good. I grow anxious for a fight."

Finished with his meditations, Akibeel stood and approached them. "You might get your wish sooner than you expect."

Rogan glared at him. "Why is that?"

"Amazarak's forces regularly attack us," Akibeel said. "But with the exception of what happened on the beach, they have left us alone since your arrival. We are overdue for an assault. I fear that they will try again before we ascend the mountain. If so, our numbers may dwindle long before we even reach the top."

"So be it." Rogan swung the hammer. "I would welcome an attack."

Akibeel didn't respond.

Asenka lay with Rogan again that night, while Javan and Zenata grew closer, as well, telling each other secrets of their childhoods. The Kennebecks and Asenka's warrior women slept as much as possible, reserving their energies in preparation for the assault.

Akibeel heard Javan and Zenata speaking, soft and low, but their words weren't of passion. He heard the girl ask,

"What are the Thirteen?"

Javan dutifully replied, "One of the stories I heard at school was that they are what remains from a previous universe. You see the sky, full of stars that goes on forever?"

"Yes."

"Story was that the ultimate God, the creator of all others and of this cosmos, destroyed a previous universe to make this one. I don't comprehend how, of course. But the yarn goes that the Thirteen are all that remain of that original universe, thirteen entities with different desires for this world."

The girl lay silent for a bit before saying, "I wonder why the God of creation allowed such things to live."

"He must have a reason. Either that or those that know of the Thirteen are lying or that some force talking to the Thirteen lied to them. They say the ultimate negative force in the universe is a liar."

"One of these Thirteen, Croatoan, or who was it?"

"Meeble. Croatoan. Different names for the same swine."

"He is at the top of the mountain?"

Javan cleared his throat a little. "Supposed to be, but I think he isn't there, at least not yet."

"Why?"

"If Meeble was, why wait? His servants cause chaos, and he loves that, I suppose, but if he were here, he'd be on a rampage, no waiting."

Akibeel retired to his lodge, and though his eyes were closed, too, the old shaman did not sleep.

Instead, he traveled the astral plane.

What he saw filled him with dread, and when he returned to his body, he still could not sleep.

He shivered silently, wrapping his arms around his legs and drawing his knees up close. Then he rocked back and forth.

For Akibeel, the dawn was a long time in coming, and when the sun finally rose, it brought no warmth.

Dawn came early for the others, as well. They rose quickly,

ate a brief breakfast, and then made their final preparations. As they packed supplies for the trip, Akibeel pulled Rogan aside.

"I traveled last night," the old man whispered. "And I am afraid. I fear we will lose this battle."

"Why?"

"Because Amazarak's forces also make preparations and their numbers far outweigh ours. They are stronger. I fear my people will lose strength during the ascent. The mountain will shatter their resolve. Croatoan exudes fear like an aura. It permeates the atmosphere at the summit."

Rogan grinned. "Let us be honest. Many of your tribe will probably weaken just from the climb alone. You're not mountain folk. You are forest dwellers."

Akibeel appeared unfazed by the veiled insult. "It is not a sheer climb, but a gradual one, for your information. My people could eagerly face and best Amazarak's soldiers if that were the only obstacle. But as I said, fear is in the air. And it is not his human followers that I am concerned about. There are others, like the beasts you saw in the vision. The hairy giants."

"The ape-men. But you said there were only a few dozen."

Akibeel nodded. "Aye, there were. But there are more of them now. Last night, I saw many more pouring from their caves. I do not know how their number could have grown so quickly."

"I think the spirits screw with your head. No matter." Rogan shrugged. "They can bleed and die, yes?"

Akibeel nodded again. "Everything can die, Rogan. You just have to know how to kill it."

Rogan clapped the shaman's bony shoulder. "That's the first sensible thing you've said since we met you on the beach. Leave the ape-men to Javan and I, and to Asenka's females. And after we've finished with them, and their blood melts the snows, we shall see if this Croatoan can perish as well."

They rejoined the others. Akibeel pulled his cloak

tighter about himself. Rogan joined the procession of fighters arming themselves. He selected his sword, a quiver of arrows, and a bow. Javan approached, elbowing his way through the crowd, and extended a flask of water. Rogan drank deeply.

Javan said, "We have a long trek ahead of us, sire."

"Yes," Rogan agreed. "And when we are done, an even longer journey awaits us. Let's get on with it. I have had my fill of this village."

Suited up, armed, and ready, the small Kennebeck army departed the forest and headed for the low plain beneath the mountain. Asenka's warriors flanked the troops on both sides. Akibeel and six braves led the way, followed by Rogan, Javan, Asenka, and Zenata, and then the rest of the force.

All of them felt eyes on them as they left the shadow of the forest, as if the very trees were watching them leave. Somewhere above the leaves, a great bird cried out, its screech echoing across the land. As the party emerged onto the plain, a dark shadow raced across the countryside. They cast their gaze to the sky, but it yawned, empty.

"Croatoan?" Javan whispered.

"Nay," Rogan said. "That was the work of the others— Karac and his ilk."

"The ones who usurped your former kingdom," Asenka said, surprised. "Then indeed, their reach is strong."

"Aye, least that is my feeling," Rogan agreed. "Enemies in front of us. Enemies to the rear. All we can do is to carve our way from the middle."

They continued on their way. The sky remained vacant, save for the blistering sun.

At a resting point, Rogan sagged wearily, collapsing atop a broad, flat rock. He stared into the sun and blinked. Javan noted his uncle's weakness, but knew better than to ask what ailed him. Asenka, however, knew no such tact.

"Do your eyes start to fail you, old one?"

"I need no eyes to make you scream, woman," Rogan muttered. "But my sight is fine. Thank you for asking. It's these visions I can't abide. They've started again, as we trekked, flooding my mind. I see things like they are remembered in a dream. I see old, black skinned people, working magic."

Javan stretched his arms high. "Perhaps these are the ones guiding the evil Karac."

"He probably doesn't think himself evil but that doesn't matter. But I was never given to visions before," Rogan said. "I don't understand why they occur. What's their source? Mine is the way of steel and blood, not soothsaying and reading fortunes. Why am I afflicted with these visions now?"

Akibeel sipped water from a flask and sighed. "Your enemies taunt you. Perhaps they cannot reach you this far and wish to draw you back to your kingdom? So they send you these visions as a means of doing just that."

"I concur," Javan said. "All the more reason to see this business atop yonder mountain finished."

"A righteous god might warn me, not taunt me." Rogan closed his eyes. "I see great peril, boy. These dire folk have made Albion murky to my mind. Algeniz..." His voice trailed off. Rogan arose and walked away.

Zenata and Asenka turned to Javan.

"Who is Algeniz?" Asenka asked.

"His youngest daughter," Javan said.

He stood up and motioned for them to stay. Then he approached Rogan and casually offered him a skin of wine. Rogan muttered no thanks, but accepted it just the same. He drained the small skin in one long swallow and tossed it aside, then stood silently. Javan cleared his throat.

Rogan glared at him. "Are you awaiting a tip?"

"You mentioned Algeniz, sire. Have you seen some new evil regarding her?"

"I have seen what Karac has in store for her."

"But she is just a child."

"That doesn't matter to him. All of them, all of your cousins, are in peril."

"All of them?"

"Erin has escaped his touch. I saw her escape in the horror that was the sacrifice of my grandchild. It was at the place of the gods on the river Severin."

"Where the giant stone blocks are erected?" Javan asked.

Rogan nodded. "I saw the wizard and his mate, dressed in dusty clothes, with Rohain's wife, Darva. She was tied down to the main sacrifice slab. Her belly was great with child, my grandchild. Erin, my daughter, was tied nearby. As the sun rose, the incantations to Damballah began. It was so real, Javan. I could see Erin's strawberry blonde hair blowing in the breeze. I could smell her scent—a scent I have known since the day she was born."

"Perhaps it was not so, sire. Perhaps this is just your imagination. Waking nightmares; I have heard tell of such a thing during my time at the university."

Rogan exploded. "Why would I dream of that bastard priest cutting the baby from my daughter-in-law's belly? Why would I envision Damballah himself descending from the sky and feasting on the life of my grandson, placed in a burning censure?"

The rest of the party glanced over at them and muttered nervously amongst themselves. Zenata took a step forward but Asenka pulled her back. Rogan towered over Javan, his muscles taut and coiled. He shook with rage. But Javan held his ground, his voice calm and assured.

"They say that sometimes things of this nature are your inner self trying to tell you something."

"Bah! I am a barbarian, boy. I know not of such silliness. I know what I see and feel what I can touch. These visions are real. Just as real as those corsairs we fought. I saw that bastard Karac, disrobing, planning to bed Erin amidst the grisly bits on the altar!"

"But sire, you said Erin escaped?"

Rogan nodded. "Escape she did, but that still doesn't make the offense any slighter. She fought him, by Wodan! She truly was my daughter. A great son she would have made."

"You speak of her in past tense."

"She kicked the usurper and jumped into the raging waters of the Severin. Then the vision faded."

Javan looked thoughtful. "Many have swam the river and survived, Rogan."

"True enough. Not many, but some. The vision didn't show me her fate; if she is dead, then good for her. She died with honor."

Javan did not reply.

Akibeel called to them. "We have a long journey, friends. We must be moving on."

Rogan did something Javan seldom saw him do. He trembled. It lasted but a few seconds, but the sight filled Javan with dread. He'd seen his uncle slay families; slaughter entire villages. He knew Rogan's capacity for violence and destruction. But never had he seen the former king express the emotions so clearly displayed on his face at that moment.

Rogan ground his teeth and stalked across the plain. After a moment, Javan followed him. They took their places in the rest of the procession, and neither man spoke.

Hours passed as they left the plains and hiked through the foothills at the base of the mountain. Well trod paths gave way to feral, tangled wilds. Only a single footpath cut through the greenery, wide enough only for a single person at a time. The party walked in silence. Rogan kept his hand near his sword hilt; his keen eyes observed all. The air hung silent and still. The only sound was the gnats buzzing in their faces and ears. There were no birds or squirrels or other creatures, but dozens of black butterflies fluttered through the weeds and clung to the vines. Their numbers increased as the group rounded a curve between two hills.

"They are beautiful," Zenata breathed. "I loved butter-flies when I was a little girl, but we never had black ones in our country."

"I would like to see your homeland," Javan told her, watching the insects.

Zenata smiled. "Perhaps you will, one day."

Meanwhile, Akibeel had halted in the middle of the slim trail. Ahead of them were two bluffs. The path disappeared into a small gap between them.

Rogan grew impatient. "Why have we stopped, old man?"

Akibeel's expression was grave. "We must depart this way and go through the forest now."

"But the path circles to the right and goes up into the higher ground. Why do we trek off of it?"

"We cannot go that way," the shaman said.

"Donkey dung!" Rogan shoved past him and continued down the trail. This caused a stir of excitement among the Kennebeck. Several of the braves nudged each other and muttered among themselves. They repeated a single word, "Itzpapaloti!"

Javan hurried to catch up to his uncle. "Sire, the word means…"

Rogan spun around. "I've spent enough time in the lands of the south, boy. I'm not a complete fool."

Asenka stepped forward. "Well, would you care to translate for those of us who didn't spend time in Ol-mek-Tikal?"

Rogan peered into the vegetation. It was full of the fluttering insects.

"Itzpapaloti means 'obsidian butterfly'. Correct, Javan?"

"Good show, sire," Javan said.

Rogan frowned. "Two things trouble me about this."

"And they are?" Asenka asked with a wry smile.

"One, that the Kennebeck know a word from a distant tribe and culture. And two, that they seem afraid to tread on the black butterflies. Have you noticed?"

"I would guess," Javan said, "that most of these primitive cultures have had some interaction, sire."

"Akibeel," Rogan grunted, "let us continue."

Shaking his head, Akibeel stood his ground. His tribesmen followed his example.

"I told you, we cannot go this way. The itzpapaloti are harmless, but sacred."

Rogan's voice dripped with scorn. "Your people worship butterflies?"

"No," Akibeel said, "but neither do we harm them. They are gatekeepers. They show the way to the Witches Gulch."

"Gatekeepers, huh?" Rogan mumbled. "Maybe that is who fucks with my head from afar. Rat bastard."

A large butterfly hovered in front of Rogan's face. He swatted it with his hand, causing an outburst from the Kennebeck warriors. The insect fell to the ground. Rogan raised his boot heel.

"Caution, sire," Javan warned.

Rogan ignored him. "What is this Gulch?"

"It is haunted by a spirit," Akibeel said. "We do not go there."

"And you didn't think to tell us of this earlier, before we set off on this expedition?"

"There was no need," Akibeel explained, "for as I said, we do not go there."

"Need? We *need* to reach the top of yonder mountain. The path goes upward. To pass through the forest adds time—time that Javan and I do not have. Tell me, what sort of ghost haunts this gulch?"

"The ghost of a great snake. Their kind used to roam free over these lands. A tribe far to the west built a great mound in its likeness, so that none would ever forget. But they do not exist anymore. This shade is the last; a cursed reminder of what once stalked this land."

Rogan stared at Akibeel, his expression one of disbelief.

"The ghost…of a snake?"

The shaman nodded.

Rogan threw his head back and laughed. Then he strode forward.

"Come," he shouted without looking back. "I shall lead us through the pa—"

His voice trailed off.

Black smoke poured from the gap between the bluffs. It swirled and coiled, forming into a shape. Gasping in terror, the Kennebeck warriors fell back, fleeing down the path. Akibeel thrust out his arms and beseeched them to stand their ground. They ignored his commands. Some of them dropped their weapons as they fled. Asenka's archers shoved past them and stepped forward, following Javan, Asenka, and Zenata as they ran to aid Rogan.

The smoke coalesced, becoming solid. It took the form of a giant serpent, twenty feet long and as thick as four stout men. The phantasm slithered not on the ground, but through the air.

Silent, Rogan drew his sword.

Javan reached back and fixed an arrow. Asenka and Zenata did the same. The scrambling Kennebeck tribesmen stopped and turned, unsure whether to flee or wait for the outcome.

Rogan stayed where he was, watching the snake in amazement. "It's as big as the pythons found near Luxor. Longer and thicker, too, I reckon."

Akibeel and his warriors shrank away as the snake floated closer. The beast did not strike. A long, forked tongue flickered from its mouth. Sunlight glinted off its black scales. The creature moved in silence.

Rogan strode forward, his sword at the ready.

"Sire," Javan shouted. "You might not want to attack that thing as such."

"What have I to fear," Rogan seethed, staring down the hovering serpent. "It moves and breathes. Therefore it can be killed."

Howling, he ran forward. The snake twisted in mid-air. Its head reared back to strike, but Rogan was quicker. His broadsword whistled as he swung it.

"Wodan!"

Javan, Zenata, and Asenka all gasped.

The blade passed through the snake as if it were air. Rogan stumbled forward. The snake's head darted for him, fangs bared. Rogan side-stepped the strike, and Asenka's bow-women let loose a volley of arrows. The missiles also passed through the snake without harming it.

Javan reached into his quiver and selected a silver-tipped arrow. Even as Rogan prepared to swing again, Javan's bow sang out. His aim was true. The silver arrowhead flashed through the air, and as it struck the serpent's form, the creature turned to smoke again. Slowly, the gas-like form dispersed until there was nothing left.

Panting, Rogan glared at his nephew.

"Silver?" he asked.

"Indeed, sire." Grinning, Javan retrieved his arrow. "Silver; the bane of creatures such as that. I retrieved it from the weapons that washed ashore after our encounter with the corsairs."

Scowling, Rogan sheathed his sword.

"Do not be angry with your nephew," Asenka teased. "You cannot slay them all."

Ignoring her, Rogan turned and started towards the gulch.

"We go this way. Akibeel, round up these worthless dogs and bid them to follow, or I will slay you all—and I won't need silver to do it."

He stalked up the trail, disappearing into the gulch. After a moment's hesitation, the others followed. They continued on their way, with Rogan now on point. Asenka, Zenata, Akibeel, and Javan followed closely behind him. The others lagged, as afraid of the barbaric foreigner as they were of the pass.

"Why do you favor such a large sword?" Akibeel asked Rogan. "I watched you wield it, during your fight with the snake spirit. A smaller sword might be better for a man of your years."

Rogan patted the giant broadsword's hilt and shrugged. "It cuts what I like and I cannot fail to slay what I hit."

Akibeel glanced at the weapon. "Admittedly, I do not know much of your swordplay, but surely, a lighter blade would be as effective?"

"For a man my age, wizard? The day I cannot lift my sword will be the day I take up a knife and place it in my own heart."

"Granted," Akibeel said, hiding a grin amongst the withered crevasses of his face. "But such a massive weapon must surely have disadvantages."

"So say you." Rogan stopped and withdrew the sword. He handed the blade to Akibeel, who nearly dropped it. "You see the craftsmanship? You feel the weight?"

"It is heavy," the shaman agreed.

Rogan snatched it back from him and held the sword high, letting the sun dance on its sharp edge. "It's heavy indeed. I can rely that it will not break in the heat of battle, and if it does, then I'm probably battling something out of my league, and will never live to contemplate it anyway. A smaller sword can break or perhaps not cut with the force I may put to it. It will strike steel or rock and shatter. Not so with this blade. Plus, it was blessed by a crazy assed wizard near my homeland. It isn't enchanted, but it makes me sleep better."

Akibeel smiled. "And you cannot understand why I need your aid in the fight against Amazarak? Harken to this, Rogan: I need an unbreakable weapon, one accustomed to war, one used to fighting."

Sheathing his broadsword again, Rogan threw back his mane of gray hair. "You fancy me as your sword of power against Amazarak and his dark god of the Thirteen? Then you are a fool. I have said before that I know no magic."

"You will."

They started to walk again. Emboldened, the Kennebecks followed closely this time, watching their leader arguing with the barbarian king.

"That's where you are wrong," Rogan said. "There are no damned wizards in my former kingdom of Albion. Do you want to know why?"

Akibeel nodded. "Why?"

"Tell him, Javan."

Javan cleared his throat. "There are no wizards in Albion because King Rogan had them all executed after he seized the throne. Those who escaped the first round with the gallows fled the kingdom and never returned."

Akibeel laughed. "None of their apprentices were angry or sought revenge?"

"No," Javan said. "We killed them, too."

"Magic is not for man to trifle with," Rogan muttered. "I have seen great evil in my life. Evil men sowing evil deeds all in the name of evil magic. I would that it was all gone from this world. Such things, demons dancing with men, will bring about the end of our age. Mark my words. We shall all drown in a flood when the gods decide to wash the evil stain from the earth."

Akibeel nodded. "You are wise for a barbarian."

"And you are brave for a skinny wizard. Your mouth is a confident one. Be careful it doesn't overestimate my civility. And when this business is done, if you accompany us to Albion, you will see firsthand what I do to wizards. It will be a bloody day indeed."

"You say you saw them perform a ritual," Akibeel said. "In your vision—one was concerning your grandson? Did you witness other acts?"

The hulking barbarian walked away from them and ducked behind a boulder. Soon, they heard urine splashing off the rocks. Then Rogan broke wind.

Javan whispered, "I believe that is his way of saying he

does not wish to discuss it."

"But," Akibeel insisted, "perhaps I can understand it better if he tells us."

"He witnessed many dire things in these visions that plague him. I beg you, Akibeel, do not press him, at your own peril."

Akibeel nodded. "I understand. Thank you for the warning."

Rogan rejoined them and they continued through the gulch. Coming out on the other side, they started up another hill. Short, stubby trees grew crooked on the hillside, their roots grasping desperately at the rocky soil. As they passed by one, Javan stopped, spying something that made him frown in concern.

Rogan breathed hard. "This is rugged country, eh, Javan?"

When his nephew didn't respond, Rogan turned. Zenata and Javan stood side by side just off the path, staring intently at a scraggly tree. Javan ran his fingers over the rough, grey bark. Zenata clutched his arm. The youth seemed oblivious to her presence.

Rogan shoved past the rest of the party. Akibeel and Asenka followed him.

"Your nephew admires trees?" Asenka teased. "What kind of mate will he make for Zenata?"

Ignoring her, Rogan shouted, "Javan! Are you losing your grip?"

"Not a bit, sire. See these marks high in the trunk of the tree?"

Rogan frowned. "Not really."

"Look," Zenata pointed. "There are deep slices in the bark."

Rogan studied them. "Awfully high for an axe, no?"

"These marks never made a break inward in the bark," Javan said. "These cuts are perfect. Meticulous. They form a word in the Kennebeck tongue."

"And what does it say?" Rogan asked.

Javan did not answer. Akibeel responded for him.

"Croatoan," the old man whispered, shuddering. "It says Croatoan."

8 THE ASCENT

THE DAY GREW shorter as they made their way through the foothills and arrived at the base of the mountain. The shadows lengthened and the sun began its descent. A few of the braves scouted ahead, cautiously searching for a safe spot to bed down for the night. The rest of the party moved slowly upward along a narrow footpath that wound through crevices and around boulders. They had traveled far and were growing weary. The mountain itself was oppressive. The air felt heavy. Sullen.

As darkness descended, Rogan stared up at the mountain's peak, still a long distance away. "I'd eat a centaur's arse for a gelding mount right now."

"The ride would do you no good," Akibeel said. "Animals—especially beasts of burden and other tamed creatures—do not like being in the shadow of this place. They would flee, and you would end up on foot anyway."

The scouts returned, reporting a small canyon with a narrow but swift-moving stream half a mile ahead. The group made haste to the site, and as the first stars came out, they made camp. Rogan cautioned them against making a fire. Instead, they huddled close together, ate hardtack and dried fruit, washing the rations down with water from the stream. One of the women killed two small hares. The rabbits were cut up and divided amongst the group. They ate the morsels uncooked, relishing the burst of energy the raw meat gave them. There was little conversation; no stories or songs or merrymaking. Weary from the march, the group turned in early. Rogan ordered four guards posted, one at each end of the camp, and selected four other men to re-place them halfway through the night.

Several warrior women bedded down beside the Kenne-beck braves. Zenata joined Javan and Asenka lay with Ro-gan, but none of them felt amorous. Instead, they merely slept—comforted by the presence of another. This close to the mountain, Amazarak's presence weighed over them all like a shroud, as dark and pressing as the night itself.

Despite the oppressive atmosphere, Asenka squirmed next to Rogan, pushing against him.

"It is cold here in the shadow of the mountain," she purred. "Make me feel warm, old man."

"Enough," Rogan growled, not even bothering to roll over and face her. "We need our strength for the task ahead. When we're finished, I'll rut with you in the battlefield's gore, if you like, before I leave."

"Do you flatter all your lovers this way?"

"Only the ones I like."

They fell silent for a while. Asenka shivered in the cold. Her eyes were drawn to the dark mountain, its peak hidden beneath ugly gray clouds. When she spoke again, her voice was soft.

"Do you fear what lays ahead, old one?"

Rogan did not answer her. When Asenka poked him, he snored.

Shortly after the second guard shift took their posts, the sen-tries were attacked. The entire camp roused from its trou-bled sleep as inhuman growls filled the air around them. Dozens of warriors scrambled to light torches or take up arms. Javan sprang up, bow in hand. He glanced at Rogan, who was already on his feet, naked, sword in hand. He shoved past Javan to the place where the sentry on duty lay still.

The moon spilled some light on the scene, but a few meager torches added to the view. A brave's head had been crushed on the crown as if a huge rock had smashed his cranium.

Javan knelt by the body, trying to determine what had happened, when out of the brush an enormous shadow divided the dim light and struck the warrior next to Rogan. The victim's skull cap pulped like a stomped melon and he bit his tongue off before toppling over in the grass. Instinct took over and Rogan swiped twice into the darkness with his sword. Something resisted his blow, but he felt the weapon sink into the obstruction, then fall through. Rogan quickly parried, kicking blindly, and then stabbed forward. A great howl rang out and a thunder of movement trampled around them all. Asenka and Zenata fired arrows blindly in to the trees. Soon, there was silence again.

"Get the torch over here, damn you," Rogan barked as a short man with a clubbed foot shined light over the dead warrior. "That man is already dead. It will do him little good!"

The brave, dumbfounded, looked at Rogan and said, "That could have just as easily have been you."

"And yet, it wasn't," Rogan sneered.

On the ground lay a long arm, covered in hair, oozing blood from the top joint. Rogan knelt, examining the severed appendage as the natives gibbered amongst themselves. Akibeel stood beside him, frowning.

Rogan looked up and said, "What manner of beasts are these ape-men? The arm is long, like a man's, only hairy and look here! It sports six fingers."

Javan audibly counted the digits and then shook his head. "Six it is, sire."

Asenka folded her arms under her one breast and sighed. "Truly a brilliant boy, Rogan."

The barbarian quipped, "Why is it you are here, again?"

The natives motioned further into the brush and the torches led them to their discovery. Eerie shadows were cast as the light washed heavy over the gigantic body of a wounded humanoid beast, missing an arm. It crawled and shuddered, clearly dying of blood loss. When it turned to face them, they saw many wounds in its belly and chest.

Rogan looked the dying creature in the eyes and then snatched a spear from the grip of a Kennebeck brave. With no fear, the old man leapt onto the calves of the beast and drove the spear into the area near its heart. With a roar that sent birds and braves to flight, the beast died. The old man stepped off the beast and took a few heavy breaths.

Zenata whispered, "Rogan struck home well with his blows. The spear was overkill."

"It is dead," Rogan said amid getting his breath back. "The dying is all that counts."

Indeed, the king's blind blows had sliced the belly open. Loops of intestines protruded from the beast's midsection. The blood smeared the trees thereabouts, painting a gory scene for them to see. The remaining braves and two women watched Rogan as he gestured toward Javan. The youth threw him a blanket and the old man wiped blood from his legs.

"Does he intend to eat this beast's heart, as well?" Asenka asked.

Akibeel nudged past them and looked at the dead creature. He seized the guts in his hands and drew them to his face. A few of the Kennebeck natives vomited at this action and even Rogan grimaced.

Javan said, "Perhaps these folk are privy to this man telling of his reading, not always seeing his methods up close?"

Rogan sighed. "Let us hope they hold their guts, son."

"It is as we feared," the shaman said. "These are the children of the mountain."

"Children?" Rogan laughed. "By Wodan and Rhiannon! If these are the children…"

Akibeel chanted, "These are what Croatoan has bred with our women and his own evil over the years. This is but one reason why Amazarak kidnaps our women."

Rogan frowned. "And you needed to burrow your nose into their innards to discover this?"

"I needed to be sure it wasn't some trick."

"What an abomination," Asenka declared and placed her hand on Rogan's left bicep. "That is the fate of any woman caught by this creature. That is why I must slay Amazarak!"

Rogan grunted, staring at the oversized visage, matted with hair. "The face is almost human. This is what came of the ravaging we saw from the damned red apes in the caves?"

Akibeel frowned and nodded weakly. Rogan sensed he was lying, but this was a learned lie. Akibeel's lie was to his own folk. He arose from his knees, dropped the guts, and walked with Rogan and Javan a few feet before whispering, "Amazarak may be breeding these women with the red apes from an age before our time, but I dare not acknowledge more than this. My folk are a feared lot and would tremble at a great evil."

Rogan chuckled, still full of grimness. "Wodan! Greater evil than breeding with beasts?"

Akibeel sighed, a tremble in his tone. "There are worst things than to breed with beasts, King Rogan."

Rogan shook his head in disbelief, but didn't press the matter. "I wonder why these red apes serve Croatoan."

"Perhaps they have no choice."

Rogan looked at the top of the mountain, wreathed in an emerald glow at regular intervals and nodded. "You are right, dammit. It is as if he captures the sun and uses it at night."

It took another full day and a few more attacks by the hirsute creatures before they reached the highest point of the mountain. Rogan could see the cresting off point and in the distance in the daybreak, a circular lodge made of red material.

Pointing back, Rogan noted, "I see the word Croatoan marked in these trees as well."

Javan nodded but kept his eyes forward. "Yes, sire."

"Always from this direction," Rogan said. "As if it were coming from this way."

Javan sighed and then frowned. "This is true."

"Why have we met no greater resistance?" Rogan snorted as Javan made sure the braves took up defensive poses. "A few of those six fingered, hairy big footed beasts, but that's all."

Akibeel shook his head as they journeyed farther into the area full of tiny tents. There was no sign of life. When they stood at the edge of the community, they could see the mouth of a cave behind the red lodge and bodies strewn all over.

"Dozens of them," Javan said, but no one went forward.

A gravelly, high pitched roar echoed from the edges of the clearing and everyone took up defensive positions. Javan saw Rogan grip the spear the old king used as a cane, thinking another of the hairy giants was about to attack. Out of the bushes leapt two large feline creatures, striped and bearing enormous fangs.

Rogan and Javan dived to one side as one of the beasts was on one of the Kennebeck savages, ripping into the belly of the man in an instant with his saber-like teeth. Before even Javan could draw an arrow, the savages themselves brandished their new weapons with steel tips and filled this tiger full of arrows. Rogan tried to get at the other one who was ravishing another small native, but the spears forged by he and Javan filled this giant cat as well.

"Damn, Javan, these savages fight well after all. Our training had some effect. I half expected them to run away. Perhaps their real colors come out when personally threatened, eh?"

The shaman took a few shaky steps, knelt by the body of the first big cat and took the knife Javan made for him to the beast's mouth. "The Kennebeck will fight, Rogan. They are simple folks, but this is their world and their land."

Akibeel worked hard and Rogan could see what he was after. The barbarian knelt and helped the thin shaman extract the sabers from the mouth of the fallen tiger. Akibeel gouged with a knife and Rogan gripped the long sabers. His great arms flexed large and he ripped the teeth loose.

Javan stared at the mountain top, pulsing green every so often, and then turned his attention back to the distant cave opening. Akibeel and Rogan removed the other set of sabers from the second dead tiger, never taking their eyes off the red lodge.

"This other wizard, this shaman, Amazarak?" Rogan questioned. "He's within the lodge?"

Akibeel sighed, looked at a large tree that faced the red lodge and dropped his buckskin tunic. He offered Rogan the four long sabers taken from the tigers and said, "Crucify me, King."

"What say you? Are you mad?" Rogan snapped.

Akibeel lay flat on the tree facing the lodge and put out his arms. "Hurry, my Lord. The game is almost ready in the dawning light. Look! My nemesis is at his power already! Hurry!"

Rogan held the spikes and looked at the red lodge. A great light appeared within and they all could see the shadow of a figure hanging by the pectorals in a ceremony much like Akibeel performed earlier in the week.

"Don't wait, crucify me!" Akibeel implored Rogan as the barbarian's eyes widened...for the corpses surrounding the red lodge began to move...stand up, rotten flesh and all, and brandish their weapons of steel. Many of these beings sported extra limbs.

"Surely this Amazarak sold his brothers out?" Rogan muttered, trying to comprehend what he saw.

Javan looked at these warriors keenly, as they brandished daggers and other knives in the extra limbs sprouting from just beneath their armpits. "These extra limbs seem full grown, like those from another person."

Rogan swore and stared at Javan. "You mean to say this Croatoan stuck extra arms on these men like a doll-maker?"

The line of four-armed warriors waved their weapons and Javan simply nodded.

The Kennebeck planted a wall of spears behind them, blocking their exit. The tips of the fence of spears gleamed in a ring.

Rogan sized up their enemies as the small army of zombies took up position around the lodge. Their thin frames turned dark every so often as the lodge oozed scarlet light at regular intervals.

He looked at Akibeel, spreading himself on the trunk of a tree—*like a filthy whore on a bed*, he thought. Rogan rolled the spiked sabers from the maw of the tiger in his palms and frowned.

"Javan, assemble the Kennebeck bowmen in a half-circle and cover the clearing." He leered at Asenka and Zenata. The women held the short swords awkwardly. True, they were used to fighting with their knives and bows, but not a longer weapon. The four-armed warriors truly inspired fear, he understood. Rogan instructed Javan and the women, "If any of our heroes run from the sight, shoot them yourself."

Javan watched Rogan place an ivory saber over the wrist of Akibeel. Rogan hesitated, seeing a wound already there, as it'd happened before. Javan urged him on with a hearty shout of, "Aye, my king!"

As Javan directed the savage bowmen to aim their metal tipped arrows at the small force of risen dead, Rogan looked into the eyes of the shaman. Still, he didn't stab the saber down.

Akibeel begged him, "Crucify me!"

"This is foolish talk, old one. What is to stop me from cutting those dead ones apart, entering the lodge, and ripping Amazarak's heart out?"

"You will never touch him without me, Rogan. I will take the fight to Amazarak in the spirit realm! This is where I will be at your side!"

"You mean I can't just cut his heart out?" Rogan asked, flummoxed, still hesitating with the handle of his sword over the saber. His blue eyes stared at the force of freakish men who stood, waiting, not attacking.

"There is a great force about his presence in the lodge, I am sure of it. You will never touch him without my help. He has stolen the souls of these men for a greater purpose." The strained cords of the ancient man were emphatic. "Amazarak uses the souls for greater magic within the lodge. Whatever that form is, destroy it before the shaman himself. His tricks to the eyes will mean naught in the end. Destroy his means of power and he will fall! *Crucify me*! Let us go to war!"

With a grunt, Rogan drove the saber through the wrist of Akibeel. The shaman's dark eyes flared and froze in that manner. Very little blood emerged and that did surprise him. Rogan glanced at the red lodge and saw the aura increase. He took another saber and savagely stabbed it through Akibeel's other wrist. The shaman groaned almost in ecstasy. That disturbed Rogan a tad as he knelt and nailed Akibeel's feet into the tree as well. Akibeel chanted and hissed, his eyes rolling back in his skull.

When Rogan joined the large force of Kennebeck braves, he looked at Javan. The young man surveyed the area and gestured his bow at the undead around the lodge. "Why do they not attack?" Javan wondered.

Rogan's eyes squinted as he drew his heavy sword. "They are a defensive force or they would be on us already. Surely, they will fall for their lord." He gave the cave mouth a glance before saying, "Perhaps something else will fight on offensive for them?" He then looked down the lines of the savages that traveled up the mountain with them. "Their hearts aren't in it. Hell, their hearts aren't beating, but getting ready to fall out their asses. Their resolve certainly isn't steel."

Asenka's knuckles were white around her short sword hilt. "My will cannot break."

Rogan raised an eyebrow. "Never did I doubt it. Still, I wonder more after what is in the yonder cave leaking green light."

All of them jumped a bit as the thud of drums resounded in their ears. Javan glanced around and then pointed. "It is from behind the lodge." They could hear the beating of these hollow drums and the echo of bestial chants. Two of the Kennebeck savages dropped their bows and ran, only to be cut down by Javan's arrows.

Rogan watched the dying men as their legs twitched and muttered, "I sense a mass desertion."

Akibeel howled, "Be strong my brothers and attack!"

"To hell with waiting. Fire!" Rogan barked and pointed with his broadsword.

The savages released their new arrows and instantly, the army of walking dead became pocked with many shafts. Several arrows found the mark in the heads of the undead, as directed by Javan. The waving arms of the undead warriors deflected many arrows as well. The young man implored them to reload and fire again. The Kennebeck braves did so quickly. Many dropped to a knee and fired at a different angle. Wavering, but not dropping, the dead men held their ground.

"Why do they not die?" Javan said, his fist striking his thigh.

"Look at their heads," Rogan pointed. "All of their scalps are gone and it is as if a maid stitched them back together. Perhaps this Croatoan has made them vessels that need no minds. They won't fall unless we cut their fucking legs off."

When several of the tall, hairy beasts stumbled out from the yawning cave, Rogan directed the troops to fire on these large creatures. The savages sporting long bows did as they were commanded. Several arching projectiles flew at the new targets. The hairy beasts, who did nothing to evade the missiles, jerked frantically, as if brawling with invisible men as they walked. The steel tips drove in deep and several of them dropped, wounded or dead. Rogan felt good to see that they could die.

Almost singing, a deep chanting voice emerged from the lodge in greater volume. The drums and chants of the beasts grew louder. Akibeel answered with his shrieking chants and his voice grew deeper as his trance world widened.

Rogan burst through the lines and shouted, "To my back, you bastards! Use your axes and let's have at these sons of bitches!" He didn't look back and expected to be obeyed when he commanded, "Form the wedge like we practiced. Hit 'em low."

With Rogan as the point, Javan to his right, Asenka at his left and the other warrior women and braves forming a wedge, they drew close together and advanced.

Swinging his heavy broadsword and cutting the knees from one of the undead, Rogan led the wedge through the line of dead sentinels. These graying men refused to leave their tight knit pattern around the red lodge at the first strikes. Wondering where the boundary for their movement lay, Rogan moved them in closer, as did the rest, swinging their new tomahawks tipped in steel. Javan, the women, and the braves chopped into those in their way, who did move to fight, but their sluggish tries were parried and met with savage blows to the legs. The multi-armed undead wobbled on their ruined legs and fought, bit, and swung, but the wedge drove through their numbers, splitting them apart easily.

Just as Rogan drew back to swing his broadsword, he saw the wide depression in the ground behind the lodge...and those making the drums sing. In a circle sat a dozen of the hairy giants with large feet, pounding the drums, facing the cave.

He swung at the nearest dead man left, slicing the right arm off and then driving the blade clean through the calf. Swiftly, he slashed the opposite direction at another one, going back for the skull. Dodging the other three arms was a new form of combat Rogan adapted to quickly. The head split like a melon, but in a scant moment, Rogan swore that no brains slopped out of the head.

Asenka and Zenata showed no fear as they used the shorter swords from the bireme to attack the dead men. They tended to work together, hitting high or low in unison as the wedge closed to a circle, their backs together. The circle then fanned out and they all sliced into their opposition.

Rogan heard a sound to make his barbarian blood turn to ice. Over the chants of Akibeel, Amazarak, and the hairy giants, he heard a hallow whoop from deep in the cave. Banishing that fear for the moment, Rogan sliced into more of the dead men. He was glad to see Javan at his side, slashing and stabbing with his short sword at the dull-eyed dead men. Javan bounced off one of the Kennebeck braves and his sword dislodged. One of the dead savages grabbed Javan by the hair and raised his right hand. Just before the fist sporting a bone-knife fell, Rogan sliced off the arm at the shoulder. Zenata threw a shoulder block into the zombie. He stumbled and ran into Asenka, who drove her sword into his cranium.

It gratified Rogan that the savages found their courage to attack as well, splitting the skulls of the dead army with ease. Since the Kennebeck greatly outnumbered these freakish zombies, the enemy was dispatched fast. Several of the Kennebeck fell, but for the most part, they fought on well. However, none of the braves dared go near the lodge.

Several of the hairy beasts from the cave reached the edge of the clearing. With wild abandoned they attacked, almost apish in their gait.

"Reform," Rogan shouted and the wedge came back, pointing into the crazed oncoming attack.

Going to their knees, many of the Kennebeck threw their tomahawks. Javan never had to train them for this exercise. With the steel insurance on the axe heads, the weapons stuck in the towering creatures. Many were of great girth and shambled forward in pain, somewhat confused that something struck a vital part, heart or head, and caused their bodies to disobey their minds. A few took blows to their thick skulls and fell, writhing. These creatures quickly took on many arrows by the Kennebeck, who grew in bloodlust as the battle went on.

Almost on cue, the dead hairy beasts sprang to life and swung their arms, braining a few braves that got greedy and went in to strike close. Rogan snarled as he directed the wedge to sweep across this bizarre force of hairy ape men. They killed that which was already dead, beheading a few, sure that a headless beast cannot fight. Soon, Rogan learned he had to extract the legs to insure this, as they kept going even with their brains disconnected.

Many Kennebeck warriors perished, but the attack and addition of the outlanders proved more numbers than the zombies could take.

Rogan peered around the side of the lodge, seeing mounds of bleached skulls by the drums and told Javan. "Arm them with arrows again. Take them from the bodies. Have them dispatch these damned giants down there. Fill them with arrows. They seem fixed on the caves."

Javan instructed the Kennebeck savages and then said, "Hear that terrible sound in the cave, sire? What is it?"

Rogan shook his mane of graying hair. "I know not, Javan. It sounds like steel on steel or the grinding of great millstones."

Zenata held her ears and said, "It is the teeth of the gods!"

Rogan frowned. "I hope not, but too much for me to think on, for sure. The giants on the drums will be easy pickings if they are so devoted to calling...whatever is in the cave. Lead these savages at them with axes after the arrows, Javan. I must go in the lodge." He hoped Akibeel would back him up as he promised.

Javan did as instructed. He led a new wedge, flanked by the women. They released a volley of arrows and started forward beyond the lodge.

9 AMAZARAK, THE DOORKEEPER, AND SHE

WITH A GREAT effort, Rogan pulled the heavy flap of the lodge open, and scarlet smoke filtered out. Out of the corner of his left eye, Rogan saw the mouth of the cave disturbed in the distance. A terrible, red colored, shambling horror appeared in the distance. It was not human in shape or gait. Deciding to let Javan and the savages have at this new arrival, he pressed on to his task at hand.

Rogan ducked and entered the lodge, ready to cut down the shaman Amazarak from his hanging pose. Indeed, the shaman hung suspended from the ceiling, pectoral muscles impaled through with bony spikes. Amazarak looked nearly to be a twin of Akibeel, only a great deal younger. A deep, throaty roar came from the shaman as a glowing, disembodied head rose from his face. It was as if a helmet overshadowed the wizard's head and had come to life. Rogan almost swung his sword and then looked down. All around the perimeter of the lodge stood tiny jars of clay. So many that Rogan froze, astonished at their number.

He moved forward and bounced back, as if a rubbery barrier unseen threw him back. Again, Rogan tried to attack and once more got repelled. He cursed the shaman and sliced with his sword, as if that could break it. To no avail, he couldn't go further.

Suddenly, in his mind, Rogan could feel the flood of a fire he feared so much. He felt the presence of magic and his barbarian nature bristled. The voice was not that of Amazarak, but Akibeel.

"I am in your mind, King of Albion! Destroy the jars. They contain the souls of those stolen. They are how he controls the hairy beasts and feeds the power beyond."

When he tried to raise a boot or move toward the jars, he found them behind the barrier he couldn't cross. Rogan cursed and tried again, then cussed himself for being foolish.

From outside the lodge, Rogan could hear panicked voices of the Kennebeck people. Perhaps Javan and the new warriors could not easily best the giants or the horror they called from the cave. He stepped forward, feeling the invisible push of Amazarak and the evil he played host to, but found himself almost paralyzed. Knowing the consequences if he failed, Rogan drew back his sword and prepared to attack the jars again. With a sizzling blanket at his back, he felt his body crushing into the invisible barrier to his front. However, the rubbery wall gave a little, bending, but not much.

Amazarak hissed from inside the disembodied face, "Look, lost King of Albion!"

Rogan stared at Amazarak, and on the shaman's belly appeared a glowing orb of green light. In this orb, he saw a vision like a moving drawing of what looked like fair Albion. He could see a bloody altar and a dark skinned, bony wizard chanting over the grisly bits of an infant.

Eyes shut tight, Rogan growled, "Begone, swine!"

"That is your grandchild, a boy, I would guess," Amazarak cooed, his voice sounding as if it were doubled in tempo. "I ate his soul up, barbarian, a soul fresh from the melting pot of the mountain all of you barbarians look to— Zenghaus! I ate him and shat him in a jar."

"Shut up," Rogan hissed, struggling, sandwiched between the invisible walls.

"Now, he is my slave, serving me with his power to help bring chaos to his realm."

Rogan's heart raged, wondering if this image was a deception, or if the shaman had really absorbed his grandson's life-force as Wodan imparted it with the spirit to fight. He waited too long and hesitated, thinking of the sacred mountain Zenghaus beyond Thule, Wodan's home. Rogan's body froze and he couldn't fight against it any more.

Akibeel shouted in Rogan's mind. "Your son Rohain still lives, barbarian! Rohain escaped the sacrifice, but your grandson did not."

Rogan felt the dour sadness of loss, a pull on the heart that made him want to drink and fight badly. He felt it seldom, only when a loved one perished, but the sensation returned now. He swallowed hard and even that took effort, still imprisoned in the forces about him.

Akibeel shouted, "Fight on! There is always hope. Reach out with your mind into the mind of Amazarak! Join with your grandson!"

"How?" Rogan groaned, confused by the words in his head.

Another voice hissed in his brain, "*WITH ME!*"

Though he closed his eyes, Rogan saw the speaker in his mind, a tall, wise figure, with features like a statue formed in the sands near Shynar. Imperious and arrogant, clothed in a cloak made of a single, seamless sheet, Rogan understood he saw the one who called himself the Doorkeeper earlier.

His mouth didn't move, but Rogan's mind wondered, *What are you doing in my head?*

Just here, waiting for you.

Can you destroy this magic force?

This isn't magic. Pissing into the wind and not getting wet, that's magic. This is just energy, like warmth from the sun yet stronger, malleable and thick.

Rogan thought, *Can we pray for moonlight?*

We? You can pray all you like, but use your brains, not your back for once.

I'll use anything to crush this bastard.

That's the spirit, no pun intended. Now then, each time you move, you fail, correct?

Fucking brilliant, Doorkeeper.

Yet, your sword falls ahead, but doesn't bounce back and hit you.

The Doorkeeper's words rang true. However, he couldn't strike out now, and the force had kept him from striking the wizard in the first place. Angry at the thought of him once able to throw his sword and be done with it all, Rogan thought, *Why do you aide me with words and not actions?*

You know the riddles of iron and steel, don't you? It is deeper than the weapon. Besides, once you finish here, I need you as a weapon inside the cave.

Rogan struggled but could not move his arms or legs. He cursed himself, for the wizard Amazarak used Rogan's passion and instincts to distract him, to trap him thus. Outside, he could hear the inhuman squeal of a horror unnamable.

Then, Rogan's eyes opened and he glanced down. He pondered the tales of iron and steel and grinned. Rogan relaxed and opened his hand. His heavy broadsword fell. As the mind of Akibeel burned around the skull of Rogan, he heard the Doorkeeper give out sarcastic applause. The mighty sword tumbled and crashed into the clay jars.

Amazarak stopped laughing as several of the jars broke. The rage of the evil shaman exploded in a howl that sent a wind around the interior of the lodge. As this wind traveled, the covering of the lodge peeled away. Rogan took a single step, froze again, unable to proceed, but saw several of the hairy beasts scattered about dead.

Rogan concentrated, uncomfortable with thinking of fighting in such a way, but felt a dim, weak part of this Amazarak. Suddenly, he realized what the shaman was. He was nothing but a crossroads, a conduit for traveling materials. When Akibeel roared in Rogan's mind, a sudden burst of light spewed from his head and into that of Amazarak. As this beam of light focused on him, the shaman swung on his supports and raged, "Good try, Akibeel! His dark gods never show him favor save for at birth. You have chosen a poor servant in this barbarian for his god never intervenes!"

The covering of the lodge blew away completely and the sun grew dim as a swirling wind of dust started to surround them. Rogan fell flat on the lodge floor, free from the invisible walls. Before Amazarak could face him, Rogan rolled over, arm slapping out lazily, disturbing the jars further. Realizing where he lay, Rogan swung down his fist, shattering a couple of the jars, and then arose. He stomped like a wobbly baby with his feet, crushing more of the jars. Amazarak reeled and screamed.

Akibeel sang out in Rogan's mind, "Destroy all of the jars, Rogan! They are the souls of the beasts he controls! Without them, he is naught. This is his reward for bringing the thing from beyond *flesh*! Croatoan has no need for souls! He wants flesh so the shaman takes the bits left over."

In a wild frenzy, gaining more power as he stomped, Rogan went feral, destroying the jars. Each time he struck, in the war against Javan and the Kennebeck folk, a hairy beast lost its resolve to fight. Whatever danced out of the cave also stopped, but he couldn't see what that was exactly.

Rogan thought the savages from down the mountain would be gone by then, but then saw his error. The force of red savages, his tribe of new barbarians, grasped the spears they left at the lip of the settlement and charged back again. Their fleeing was a ploy to draw the hairy beasts into the open and away from their drumming. The savages pierced the beasts, running them through and killed many. Those no longer under the spell of Amazarak fled into the forest.

The dark shaman came down from his perch and stood over the last jar, a tiny vessel. Amazarak scooped up this jar and ran toward the cave, howling, "That is the soul of your grandson, Rogan! Crush it and all is lost for him!"

Broke from his frenzied spell of death dealing, Rogan scooped up his sword and ran after the wizard.

When Rogan chased Amazarak into the cave, something else bolted out, passing him by at a different angle, not even looking his way. Javan saw Rogan take note of the new arrival, but didn't do a double take. Javan, nonetheless, did.

At first, he mistook the running figure for another of the hairy beasts with big feet, save for that by the breasts and anatomy tagged it as female...and the beast was hairless from the waist up. Beast? Yes, he thought as she stomped out and made a bead on their clustered group, partially human wasn't enough. Like a fawn or satyr, her lower portion curled back like a deer's hindquarters, legs ending in cloven hooves that stabbed into the ground like she held a grudge on the earth. Though her stomach looked full of squared muscles like an athlete, her breasts, though tiny, numbered more nipples than Javan could count. Her elongated head, almost horse-like, held a mouth of fangs and came crowned with long tresses, braided and waxed in long locks that extended to her waist.

While he took up his bow and shouted for the others to do likewise, she planted her hooves and shook her head about. That's when Javan saw the tail. When the thing extended out from behind her, swaying in the air, he half expected it to rattle. When the sunlight showed a gleam off its tip, a hooked sickle like that of a scorpion, Javan wished it had rattled.

At this revelation, a few of the Kennebeck turned and ran for the forest. As they ran each shouted the word "Giwaka," so that's what Javan named her. It only took a few moments as she charged forward at the few Kennebeck braves who did stand their ground to fight for Javan to comprehend the others' horror. He'd never seen a giant female satyr cannibal, nor had he heard of such a beast in his bedtime tales, but after witnessing the arrows blunt on the beast and seeing her leap onto the braves and take a bite from the face of one, he wouldn't soon forget her.

Her hooves crushed into each one as she landed, stomping through the left thigh of one brave and burying another's foot into the turf. Her long fingernails sank into the chest of the one sporting a ruined leg, as she grabbed a handful of the other brave's face, yanking him in close to bite his cheek off. All stood dumbstruck in terror as she didn't just spit out the grisly piece, but immediately went in for more mauling, the brave screaming, biting off his nose and rutting in the nasal cavity. She dropped him and came up with a gray piece of slime in her mouth -- Javan wondered if it was brain -- and sucked it in. A long tongue slathered out, forked on the ends, and she turned to the other brave in full, biting mouthfuls of his shoulder off and tearing his chest open like she opened shuttered doors of a saloon.

Asenka, Zenata, and two of their warrior women ran forward, all firing into Giwaka, and quickly following up their arrow shots with a thrown tomahawk. The arrows didn't sink in, but scratched her, annoying Giwaka, and she went low and spun all about. Javan couldn't fathom her speed...and saw the hooked tail swing out, and chop off the ankle of one of the women. As she fell, Giwaka stood again, swiped both arms out, and clocked Asenka and Zenata in the jaws, sending each woman tumbling. She then leapt onto the fallen warrior girl, hooves crushing her left kneecap and kicking her face, utterly pulping her skull, hoof cleanly passing through.

Giwaka stood atop her and roared, and Javan released his arrow. He'd waited for the moment and the shot went near to perfect. He'd seen it in his mind, the arrow hitting Giwaka, going through her open mouth and lodging into the roof of her mouth. However, the creature closed her mouth and then grinned.

"Fuck me," Javan mouthed, astonished that Giwaka caught the arrowhead in her teeth. He dropped his bow and pulled his short sword just as she charged forward. Faster than any animal he'd ever been near, Javan twisted, trying to roll with whatever she had in mind, but extended his sword, which she slapped away. That move saved his life. As the claw rushed for him, he moved and she performed an inadvertent tackle, sending Javan down, reeling.

He faced her as her legs flexed, and he felt his death draw nigh. However, a few Kennebeck braves that had courage ran forward, using the long spears, and jabbed at her breasts. These long blades did penetrate her teats and she roared. She performed an elegant kick, hopping on one hoof before extending the other, crushing in the chest of one brave, and getting her hoof caught in his ribs.

Giwaka turned to face Javan again, tail swinging about to stab through the kidneys of another brave as she tried to get her hoof free of the other like she shook off manure. Javan started to rise, but Giwaka seized him by both shoulders in a touch not unlike a dominant whore that he once bought in Irem. She brought him up with force toward her face and he'd have gotten his jaw bitten off had Asenka not leapt onto her back, a tomahawk in each hand and started to chop at the sides of her neck like a person driving nails. Giwaka dropped Javan, who immediately armed up his sword to thrust at her breasts. He found the skin tough but not impossible.

She spun, trying to shake Asenka, and Javan saw some blood rise from the repeated blows. The warrior woman on fire, she kept striking and was smiling at Javan the moment a sharp point emerged from the flat spot on her chest where a breast should be. Asenka froze, looked down, confused at the stinger point sticking from her chest a good four inches.

Giwaka snapped Asenka from her back, depositing her dead form to the dirt. In that single moment, when Zenata lost control and went after the beast with her tomahawk and a dagger, Javan saw the tail still embedded in Asenka and dove toward it. Knees in the dead girl's back, he used her as leverage as he swung the sword at the tail, chopping three times near the stinger, and cleaving into the flesh of Giwaka. Giwaka roared, slapping Zenata away, bloodying her nose, and turning fast. Javan flattened on Asenka's body, forcing more weight on the extended tail. Giwaka's own momentum ripped the stinger off, leaving it half out of Asenka's back. She screamed loud as Javan rolled off Asenka and pulled the stinger out.

Suddenly, a dozen Kennebeck braves charged Giwaka, swarming her with numbers, knocking her from her attack on Javan. Though she threw off three of them in the pile, the weight of them shocked her enough to get her from her hooves. They had her rolled over, flat, and Giwaka did a push up, rising with a half dozen on her back.

Zenata ran with a tomahawk and swung low, smashing the blade into her nose. The nose split and their eyes met. Zenata screamed and drew back, over and over, and kept hitting her in the face. She grinned, blood running into her fangs.

Javan leapt to her back and grabbed Giwaka in a head-lock, the stinger in his hand, swiping it across her throat. Giwaka grabbed back and threw Javan, ass over elbows, sending him to the flat of his back on the ground. Her hand to her throat, she looked at more blood. Head tilted, as if fascinated, Giwaka looked down at Zenata again. This time though, the one breasted girl didn't hesitate. She held the stinger Javan dropped with two hands and drove it down into the abdomen of Giwaka, splitting her open down her belly and to her pubic ridge. On her knees, covered in the blood that gushed from Giwaka, Zenata flipped the stinger about and stabbed upwards into the creature's vagina. Buried deep, she twisted and shoved it farther before falling away, bringing out loops of gore Javan couldn't name.

Giwaka wavered on her hooves, then fell, hands to her belly like she could put herself back together again.

Zenata rose up and started to stab and swipe at Giwaka's head with the stinger. She jabbed, relentless, until

Javan stood and pulled her away. He bet she stabbed Giwaka's head fifty times.

The creature fell over and exhaled loud, a final breath escaping.

Zenata fell to the ground, looking at Asenka, face down in the ground, dead. She cried and Javan knelt, holding her.

The earth shook, a little at first, then more.

Amazarak was just ahead of Rogan as they ran into the cave. Green light surged around them as they disappeared within.

They ran in several yards before Rogan stopped, realizing the lines of flashing steel covering the walls would not happen in an ordinary cave. The shaman padded away up ahead behind many squared objects as cold air surrounded Rogan. He shivered as if he had just stepped into the snowy lands of Thule. He looked behind him, still seeing the green lands and the squeals of the beast they passed. Dismissing this chill and trying to block out the humming in his mind, he cautiously moved into a larger chamber. Hardly part of a cave, this area sat as a squared room like the interior of a palace. He half expected a line of guests and foreign princes to be lined up and received.

The main background stayed grim and dark, but a green glow seeped in from various boxes. A rainbow selection of lights tapered on rectangular tablets tilted on boxes displaying symbols Rogan couldn't read. Every so often, icy chills flowed over his sweaty frame. That sensation, added to the footsteps of Akibeel and the Doorkeeper in his brain, made Rogan uneasy at the least.

Beyond these flickering boxes sat dozens of giant tubes lining the walls. Rogan guessed these were made of glass. Inside each container floated a humanoid shape, but not just human bodies. Rogan stopped, staring at the various containers, seeing hovering forms of women, children, and monstrosities unnamable. One tube contained what looked to be a female figure, however the skin ran scaly, reptilian, and the feet terminated in fins. In another cell a head was sub-divided as if two normal human children lived in the same form yet separating slowly. Yet another cell held the shape of what Rogan assumed were clots of seaweed... however this proved to be material emerging from the back of a tiny man, mercifully asleep. One container on the end hung higher than the rest, open, and fluid coated the floor. His eyes traced a trail out of the room. He wondered if that was the thing that Javan and the others fought outside.

Shaking his head, Rogan returned to the task at hand. He ran through these many containers to yet a larger room, this one with a vaulted ceiling but more natural in caves. Bizarre boxes of objects filled this place, too, and he caught a glimpse of the dark shaman. He sheathed his sword and moved in closer. More tubes continued on, and Amazarak slipped between these containers and seemed to struggle with something on the ground. When Rogan drew closer, he saw Amazarak placing a series of metallic objects on hooks attached to the wall. The shaman stepped into some form of armor, much larger than plated materials or suits Rogan had seen in his life. He paused, trying to understand what the wizard did, wagering Amazarak donned armor to try and best him in battle.

He grinned, hand returning to his sword, feeling the end of the game near.

As Amazarak closed the legs and midsection of the armor, something caught Rogan's eye. Into the interior of the cave another glowing tablet hung...no...there was no wall. Rogan squinted and took a step toward it, trying not to reveal himself to the shaman. There was no tablet on a wall glowing...but a swirling glow in mid-air, a fingerprint like smudge in reality, just hanging there like a terrible painting splattered on the air itself.

Amazarak's voice filtered out, sounding like it grated underwater. "You should not have followed me here."

Rogan drew his long blade and faced him. "You're probably right, but I ceased giving a shit a long time ago."

Several glittering lights danced on squared tables on the opposite side of the vast room. More lights flared above them, revealing even more tubes and human forms. Rogan glanced at these people, who were different than the others. Each of these bodies wore clothing. What struck him as odd was that nearly all of them were dressed alike, in garb unfamiliar to his travels around the world. The males were clad in black breeches, white undershirts, and black coats. Some still bore wide brimmed hats with metallic buckles on the hat bands. The females floated in their drab, dark gowns and pale bonnets.

The shaman moved, clumsy at first, but then with more grace in the armor that resembled shiny gray steel. The gauntlet-like hands hung at the end of the arms, each suddenly producing a razor blade three inches long. Rogan saw heavy pinchers folded backwards behind these appendages. A hinge like from a door held these items in place. The rather box-like helmet bore a series of steel spikes that closed over the shaman's face like a fly-trap plant. Steel ground on steel as the glittering giant moved toward Rogan smoothly.

When Amazarak faced him, the series of spikes covering his face slid open. These armored spikes to the sides, Rogan saw a glassy mask over a faceplate.

Then, Rogan noted the tiny jar over beside the wall where the shaman got dressed in the armor. Rogan shoulder rolled past the shaman, sliding a bit more than he wanted to on the slick floor, and came up against the wall. He seized the jar, but had no time to act...not that he understood clearly what to do with it anyway.

Gripping the jar in one hand and the handle of his sword in the other, Rogan saw the left arm of the armor flip around the pinchers on the hinge. This arm started to extend as Amazarak approached him. The aged warrior dove to the floor, feeling every joint in his body ache as the smooth floor never gave way.

Truly, it was not a wonder stupid men thought this creature a god, he mused.

"You fucking devil," Rogan spat, getting up to his knees. "Just another monster in a suit of armor playing wizard games with lives."

Rogan expected a laugh, but got none. Instead Amazarak paused and then said, "You are strange in this land, large man. Yet you dread spirits like all of the primitives in this world. It is no marvel I chose this continent for analysis, not your savage realm."

"I'm not a man of big words but I don't think you are just a rival tribesman, are you?"

Amazarak made no move to get to Rogan. He replied, "You are correct. However, you appear to be a person of action. I shall give you some." The creature turned and touched a gleaming button on a table.

The steel floor under Rogan's body boiled and came alive with a million sparks. Jumping to his boots, still feeling the sparks, Rogan's instinct took over and he leapt onto one of the tables of glittering lights. On his haunches like a panther, Rogan faced his enemy again.

"You are not from my world," Rogan snarled, "but you are no damned god. You are flesh hiding inside that steel."

"That is wrong on a number of levels, barbarian. This…" He held up a metallic hand and flexed the fingers. "This is not steel, but I comprehend that you would see it as such. Indeed, you are wise in that I am no god, but you are mistaken on your first thought. I am from your world, but from a time far distant from yours. You could never understand my journey back in time, continually falling backwards, never able to return or go forward again."

Gripping his jar and his sword, Rogan said, "I heed not the ravings of madmen."

"But since you cannot see how to kill me, you hesitate. Death is what it is all about, barbarian. The energy of death and life is all I have to study now." He gestured at the tubes around him. "My trophies and subjects from other times, yes, I carry many with me as I travel backwards." Amazarak glanced at a small tubular spot at the back corner of the room. It was hardly large enough for a child to fit in.

"Why torment us? Go home."

"I cannot, barbarian. My great engines you hear around you are damaged and my fortress, as you may call it, can no longer travel with me. If I choose to go myself, yes, I can move on." Again, the being looked at the small closet and Rogan wondered if the creature realized he was doing it. The longing in the eyes of the shaman was real to Rogan. This creature appeared bored, if anything else, but as much a prisoner as his subjects in fluid. "Magic and science blur at times, and I have made sacrifices to try and survive, to get to other places and discovered the horror of the Thirteen, but made bargains for their goals."

Rogan jumped down and moved behind one of the tubes, surprised the floor no longer stung.

Sounding amused, Amazarak said, "You would be an interesting study, barbarian. I wonder how you would fair against others in my collection, or at an even earlier time when the ante-humans roamed the plains? You are such a fool though, to think that I wear just a suit of armor, when it's just a means to study lower forms of life. Still, it protects me from a beast like you." He glanced at the glowing thumbprint in the air. "He's coming, you know."

"Who?"

"Croatoan...Meeble...the fulfillment of my bargain. He will destroy and rip apart this realm."

"But if you are from the future, won't he stop history and change it all?"

"There are other worlds than these, different stripes and flavors, you cur. Perhaps in another time line, you and Javan are not from Albion, but men from Transalpina or long lived mercs from Shynar? Maybe in another time Karac is your son, but you love each other? Who can say?"

He had one chance as Amazarak moved forward. Rogan threw himself against one of the glass tubes. A female body sloshed about and the tube went over. It bounced on the floor and rolled. When Rogan slashed his sword down, the heavy blade made a crack in the clear material. The blade bounced up and came near to striking Rogan's chest. Suddenly, the tube shattered on the floor, spilling a yellowy fluid all over. This action made Amazarak stop in his motions. Rogan then went mad, toppling more and more of the tubes, staying ahead of the steel beast and the pinchers it waved at him.

He shoved a container with some thing that looked like a human full of budding plant fibers at Amazarak. The shaman inadvertently embraced the tube with his pinchers, crushing the clear walls and bursting the fluid all over its steel self.

"Worm." Amazarak raged and jerked in his movements. "You are a rat in my maze and there is no escape."

Rogan charged Amazarak as he tried to shrug off the container pieces. He slid forward on the slick fluid, looking for a gap in the armor to insert his blade. The metal right hand swatted Rogan and he flew back. Though he rolled with the swipe, he thought his jaw dislocated. Truly, strains of his long hair hung up in the blade tips on the gauntlet.

Flailing on the table of lights, Rogan struggled to hold the jar and the handle of his weapon. Suddenly, his mind flared, the fingers of Akibeel pushing him. Looking at a gleaming red button, Rogan put his hip on the table, thus distancing himself from the floor, and slapped the button.

The floor sizzled as the force Amazarak once employed on Rogan swept the room again. The fluid bubbled and smoked on the floor. The shaman twisted, his armor jerked and sparks flew from the back of it.

Not defeated, Amazarak took wide strides toward the table. The hinges snapped forward as the pinchers came full on. However, he then used them as a bludgeon and swung down at Rogan.

With no worry for his safety on the hot floor, Rogan leapt out of the way. His boots indeed felt the stabbing of icy daggers from the floor, but it was short lived. The metal claw smashed at the boxy table, destroying the controls and inadvertently stopping the bizarre effect.

Again, Rogan attacked. Just before he stabbed upwards with the sword, he felt the power of Akibeel guide his arm and say, "No, this way," and direct the blade away from the groin of the suit and into the backpack of the armor. Fire and sparks burst out of the armor, but Amazarak swung a claw toward him. Rogan dropped before the blow fell and rolled away from Amazarak. The armor stumbled and Rogan arose, throwing a shoulder into his enemy, barely making Amazarak stagger a little inside his armor. The shaman took a few steps and jerked in his motions, knocking over another one of the tubes. This container fell and shattered, further saturating the floor with amber fluid.

Abruptly, Amazarak was afire from the backpack and more sparks flew. Rogan stabbed at the back part of the armor again and Amazarak fell. The armor split from the front and the man inside popped out.

"Fool! This mountain is full of my power and that of the coming Meeble! Disturb it in the slightest, you savage, and we will all explode! The leak in radia…"

Rogan's howling rage cut the man off and Akibeel hummed a song in the barbarian's head. Rogan raged, saying, "The secrets of metals and of life come from Wodan, not Amazarak! This is but a demon pretending to be a god!"

Rogan dropped his blade and set down the jar. The shaman snatched up the jar and that made Rogan swear anew. He reached out and caught the shaman at last. He snapped Amazarak's wrist and then took the soul jar up again. Rogan held the jar as if it were a delicate newborn.

His heart was heavy as the words came to his mind from Akibeel, "Your grandson is dead, Rogan. His soul has no flesh to return to."

Wincing in agony at his new injury, Amazarak went to one knee. "It is too late, savage!"

Rogan twisted the broken wrist back further and a noise not unlike reeds breaking echoed briefly. "That is not important, wizard. Dying is all that really matters." He held up the jar. "His death, and now yours…"

Yanking his mangled wrist from Rogan, Amazarak scrambled away, moving like a spider toward the back corner of the room. The creature was up on its spindly legs, sucking for air, coughing.

"This is your day to die, damn you!" Rogan promised as he stood tall.

Amazarak pulled a handgrip down a notch and hissed in the mind of Rogan, "Someday I may have to die, but not at the hands of one such as you." He slipped into the closet and a clear door sealed him in tight. "Besides, you are going to die in a minute, fool. Look, Croatoan comes!"

The floating swirl grew larger and Rogan's ears popped. He drew back as far as he could to the edge of the room as the swirl increased, near to ten feet across. Rogan saw a shape forming in the glow and he felt pressure on his bladder. Having seen monsters before, he stood, set down the jar with his grandson's soul in it, and took a piss as Meeble started to become solid in the glow. Since he doubted Meeble wanted to be his friend, Rogan figured he'd rather piss before fighting his final battle.

When Meeble stepped out of the swirling glow, Rogan was glad he went, as he wanted to piss again.

10 AT WAR WITH MEEBLE

FAR MORE IMPRESSIVE than the towering, big-footed beasts outside that clearly worshiped him, Meeble stood near to nine feet tall. That came as a guess, as Rogan stood near to six and a half feet himself. Unlike those skinny, wormy creatures, Meeble had a thick, hulking body, much broader across, like a bull gorilla in the middle and thighs, but his arms hung thinner, longer, like an orangutan, looking somewhat out of proportion with the rest of him.

White fur covered his form, save for a bare portion on his chest and belly, and there the skin held a bluish tint. Rogan noted the feet of the beast held a simian touch, as they were near to hands, down to an opposable thumb. However, the hands were not unlike human ones: hairy, palms blue and clean, and yet they held a curled in dew nail, like a feline or dog. The feline features didn't stop there, for Rogan expected the face to be an apish monstrosity, but Meeble's eyes, green and striped down the middle, were set into his boxy head like a cat, drawn up in an almond shape even. Down between his eyes, an almost dainty nasal cavity snaked, and drew up like a lion's snout. The mouth wasn't jutting or catlike at all, more flat and across, akin to a cave covered by falling water, no definition.

When the head turned a little and the eyes blinked, Rogan's heart beat faster. The sides of Meeble's head sported ears, slanted and pointy, extending out from his head like a feline, and even twitching a bit. Meeble turned some, slowly, and took note of Amazarak in the booth. Some move not unlike a nod emerged from Meeble and he faced Rogan. Legs apart, he shuffled his feet a little and stood firm, stretching his limbs, not ashamed that his furry penis and balls swung from his crotch.

The thumbs on Meeble's feet tapped the floor, almost like a nervous twitch, but the rest of him didn't appear shook up at all.

As the swirling circle behind Meeble reduced to the size of a tiny foot-wide disk, Amazarak's voice cut the tension, shouting out to Rogan, "You better run, barbarian. As they say where I came from, you don't know who you're fucking with."

Rogan looked up into the face of Meeble and recalled the Nephilum, Lambach, and how big he stood. At age thirty, Rogan's army of rogues had destroyed the half breed angel's breeding domain at Baalbek, and Lambach himself… but there had been two hundred of them and one of him. Now, these odds sucked ass.

Hands gripped to fists, Rogan still leered at Meeble as he said to Amazarak, "He doesn't know who he's fucking with."

The cat eyes focused on Rogan, nostrils expanded, and one eye seemed to quiver, perhaps an expression. Meeble may have had an idea of what stood before him, perhaps even who if Amazarak fed him information, but he didn't give a damn. His mouth opened, the lips parted, and two words fell out.

"Show me."

The voice dropped like rolling boulders, raw, deep but rough and phlegmy.

Rogan showed no fear, even if he fought it down into the top of his gullet. He eyed the beast, but didn't draw his weapon. He looked for a point to strike at. The strange, curling flopping penis held an obvious point of assault for Rogan's mind.

Meeble looked about the room, perhaps taking note of the ruined tube and the armor of Amazarak on the floor. He then looked past Rogan, beyond this great cavernous room into the next.

"My way," Meeble grunted, hands flexing.

Rogan's eyes narrowed, not understanding.

"My way," Meeble repeated, hands together, almost wringing them, thumbs on his feet tapping louder.

Rogan saw the path of Meeble's look and glanced behind him at the exit. Rogan faced him anew and nodded. "I am in your way, aren't I?" he reached back and drew his broadsword. "That I am."

Meeble's mouth drew at the corners, became broader, and Rogan thought he heard a chuckle. "I am," he said, chuckled again. "I am…I am…"

When the member of the Thirteen started to move forward, Rogan reared back, came up low, and stabbed for Meeble's gut. The long arms moved fast, the hands slapping on either side of the blade, stopping Rogan's thrust mere inches from the exposed belly. Meeble's arms flexed and Rogan dropped his weight, trying to avoid the coming pull that would've ripped the weapon from his grip. Rogan's body fell between Meeble's legs and the sword slipped from the hands. A chopping shot fell toward him from the right hand of Meeble, but Rogan shifted, right into a chop of the left, but his blade pushed off on that shot, the flat of the sword helping to mute the strike. Meeble's hand didn't slap his face but bounced off his shoulder. Rogan felt like a stone block had bounced off him.

Boots up together, Rogan kicked at Meeble's balls. Though Meeble had lowered himself to strike, Rogan had failed to estimate his distance right and missed the testicles, but his boots did strike the end of the swinging prick. Meeble reacted, stepping back from him and standing up straighter. Rogan rolled and got to his knees. He could've sworn he saw the member protrude spikes for a moment then return to normal.

I grazed his manhood and he reacted, Rogan thought. *That's good news. I'll have to tell the priests back home to put that in their books.*

He started to rise and Meeble moved on him, arms up, preparing to drop a crushing blow. Rogan, still on his haunches, sprang, a shoulder block to Meeble's gut, the sword across him, jabbing at Meeble's thigh. The long arms went over Rogan, who didn't wait to see if his gut tackle had any effect, for Meeble stood and adjusted his strikes. Rogan hugged his right leg low, curled about him, and swung the sword down. While his right hand drove the blade at the top of Meeble's foot, his left forearm came up between the being's legs.

Rogan's father, Jarek, had always said there was no such thing as a fair fight. The shot to Meeble's testicles proved effective and the huge being reacted immediately, just like any man hit in such a place. He hunched over, hands to his groin, face full of pain and eyes with anger.

Though his blow to the foot hadn't landed properly, Rogan had it all planned...he rolled between Meeble's legs and would come up swinging, nailing the throat with his sword for the kill shot. Rogan did just that, somersaulting between his legs and pulling back for the deathblow. Meeble, though, let go of his nuts and boxed Rogan's ears. Feeling right away dizzy, and amazed his head didn't pop apart, Rogan found himself airborne, then slung across the room like a disk at a gaming show. Crashing into a table, Rogan took out a few of the glowing boxes and rectangular tablets with odd symbols on them. He rolled to the floor again and got up fast.

Rogan had Meeble's attention. He'd turned to block the way out, focused on Rogan alone.

As Meeble turned to face him, he sprinted to one of the tubes holding a body, wedged his sword against the wall, and pried it loose from the moorings. He threw himself against the glass, and it toppled, set to crash on the floor before Meeble. The tube hit the floor and didn't break. It rolled over and Meeble stopped it with his handish foot.

"Shit," Rogan muttered, and noted the figure inside the tube had long hair, a thick waist-belt concealing dirk handles, and a long spear at his side. The gleam of the spear made Rogan randy as he made his move.

A foot on the tube, Rogan leapt up, swinging the sword, eye level with Meeble. The strike would've been impressive had it landed. As the blade swung and Rogan flew in the air, Meeble tilted back and swiped out, backhanded. Amazed the big thing was lucky enough to slap the flat of his sword…hard enough to knock it from his grip, Rogan flew into Meeble, unarmed. Knee up, instinctually ready for the impact, he didn't strike Meeble. The right hand of the monster grabbed his left arm and the left hand drew across his body and bitch slapped him. Hard. Rogan's weight proved tough to hold with one hand and Meeble dropped him. As he fell and rolled on the floor, Rogan felt the left side of his face crinkle as if parchment had been wadded up. Tongue over his teeth, not finding any empty slots, Rogan felt the onslaught of the pain arrive and spider clawed away on the floor. Meeble's hands fell at where Rogan landed, and the being spoke again.

"Killer."

Scurrying about the fallen tube like a rat, Rogan searched for his fallen sword, and looked hungry at the spear inside the glass tube. Eyes on Meeble, the creature glared back at him.

"Not coward." Meeble breathed and might have grinned as he declared, "Killer."

Rogan thought to spout a boast, like there were plenty more like him back home, but dived for his blade.

Meeble anticipated this move and lurched toward that direction, causing Rogan to not kneel as he'd have been exposed to a punch. Though he stopped, and turned, Meeble chopped at him again. Rogan tilted his body, avoided the blow and the follow up that intended to knock his head askew. Bent, Rogan spun, did a three-sixty, and tried to dodge again, but slipped in the amber goop on the floor. Desperate, Rogan took a knee, scooped up the wet goo in his hands and threw it into Meeble's oncoming charge. The wet splashes struck Meeble's face and his arms failed to hit Rogan. He shook his head like a dog clearing water. Pleased with himself, Rogan reached and grabbed up the hilt of his sword.

With a step, Meeble bridged the gap between them and they both stood by the wall. Meeble's left foot slapped on the flat of the sword tip, and his right hand covered Rogan's on the pommel. With a fast move, Meeble yanked and the great broadsword snapped in half. Rogan let it go and squatted fast, exiting between Meeble's legs. Before he could even get clear, Meeble turned and slapped him between his shoulder blades, sending him staggering and impacting on another of the tall glass tubes. Rogan hugged the tube, this one containing a sea-weed thing. He sucked air, trying to get his wind back and quickly peeled himself free of the tube, knowing Meeble stalked him close.

Meeble swatted with both arms, smashing the glass tube asunder and Rogan moved about him, swinging a fist, punching Meeble where his kidneys should be. As the great glass beaker broke open and splashed all over Meeble, Ro-gan avoided the back swing of the creature's arm, and grabbed into the oncoming muck. He pulled whatever spewed in the tube out faster, slamming it into Meeble, who back pedaled, somewhat confused by the rush of fluid and the seaweed thing inside. Rogan grabbed a hold of Meeble's elbow and swung himself up, kicking the being in the face hard as he backed up. Rogan let go and fell into the debris, hands and boots up like a crab, watching Meeble stumble and then near to fall over the other tube. Meeble stood over the tube, both hands on it, shaking his face free.

Hardly a moment lapsed as Rogan grabbed up a hunk of the broken glass like material and ran at Meeble. Though Meeble moved, Rogan's swipe found a home, stabbing the jagged edges of the glass into the creature's buttocks. Meeble roared and something darker than blood sprang out in the white fur.

Rogan moved about the prone tube, grinning, so glad to see Meeble bleed. He took the hunk and crashed it down, breaking open the tube between them. He grabbed the spear at the side of the man in the tube and the figure in the beaker held onto it. A moment of terror grabbed Rogan, afraid this person would arise from sleep and fight him, too. However, it was a reflex and the grip of the soldier from another time dropped.

The moment was all Meeble needed to turn, grab a handful of Rogan's hair and swat him in the belly. Though he tensed up his guts, the shot hurt terribly. Rogan couldn't count the punches to his stomach he'd taken, but few as strong as that. As a youth, he prided his gut as a cast iron place almost invulnerable. Still, this strike nearly made him puke on Meeble.

He dropped the spear, still dangling from the grip of the monster, and flailed as Meeble struck him again, same spot. Again, Rogan took the shot, but the hurt made him ache all over.

"Strong man," Meeble grunted, dropping the barbarian as he reared back and aimed at Rogan's face. Rogan rolled away, pushing off with his boots on Meeble's chest, but the fist still connected with his jaw. In the air again, Rogan's eyes lit with a million stars and his head filled with craziness, confusing images of slaughtered people and burning villages in realms made of steel and glass. All of that went away as he impacted on the floor. For a moment, all went black, but his mind resisted and he turned, again hearing the voice of Meeble. "Hard man."

Meeble picked him up by the shoulders and head-butted him clean on the forehead. Once more, Rogan's head went afire with crazy pictures of the dead in places he'd never seen. The ground, once more, sobered him up.

"Iron man," Meeble mused, his voice curious.

Certain his brains had sloshed to the back of his skull, Rogan's body felt weary, and didn't respond right away when he dived between Meeble's legs, making a vain attempt at the spear.

Meeble caught his boots, held him up, and opened his mouth to speak again.

Rogan reached out, grabbed Meeble's penis, and twisted it like he broke the neck of a snake.

Meeble let him go.

Sure that the organ felt serrated in his hands when he touched it, Rogan hit the ground with his shoulders, and ignored the cry of pain from the hulking creature. Boots back on the ground, Rogan arose and ran, trying to avoid Meeble's oath of a strike, but the big thing held his manhood, groaning. Slipping past the tube in the goo on the floor, Rogan grabbed the spear. A beautiful weapon, near to seven feet in length, a bronze ball weighting it on the end, a sturdy shaft and heron feathers near the joint below the blade, Rogan liked it, a lot.

Meeble swung around, still hunched over, anger in his almond eyes.

"Dead man," he snarled.

Rogan liked Iron Man better and brought the butt of the spear about, connecting the bronze ball with Meeble's right eye. By the way the creature jerked back and shook, Rogan hit an area as good as Meeble's prick. Rogan waded in, dodging each punch or slap from Meeble's left arm with the ball of the spear higher up. Meeble held his right eye, backing away as Rogan parried him, over and over, alas, swinging the bronze ball up for another groin shot. Though Meeble angled away, he still caught a grazing and hunched over a bit...far enough, Rogan thought.

When Rogan went for the straight stab into Meeble's left eye, Meeble dropped to his ass and grabbed Rogan's legs with both of his hand-like feet. The left hand jabbed at Rogan, who instinctively brought up the spear for defense. The spearhead blade flattened on Rogan's face, smashed into it by Meeble's swat. Rogan felt his nose give and blood spewed down his mustache and beard. This didn't slow down his thinking, as Rogan's nose had been broken many times before.

Meeble's feet tightened, holding Rogan firm.

Rogan dropped the spear from defense and jabbed ahead, aiming for the eye Meeble at last revealed, blinking it many times. The beast saw the blow and jerked his body away, his grip free of Rogan's legs. The spearhead found a home, but not in Meeble's head. The blade, over a foot long, inserted into Meeble's right shoulder easier than Rogan could've dreamed. About ten inches sank in and struck bone. Rogan tried to push harder, but the agonized frenzy of Meeble sent him tumbling again, the feet, though not gripping Rogan, pushed off, knocking him down. The spear shaft, out of his grip, hung out of Meeble's shoulder, flaccid.

Boots on the floor again, Rogan glanced at Amazarak, who watched with wide eyes, hardly breathing. Rogan then advanced on Meeble, who still sat on his buttocks, fumbling with the spear. When Meeble grabbed the shaft to pull it free, Rogan leapt into the air, drop kicking the beast's hand on the shaft. The spear broke off, and the spearhead delved in deeper. Rogan fell over Meeble, who got to his knees, roaring in pain, trying to rise up again.

Up to his feet again, Rogan's legs shook. Full of battle crazy, his very being felt a wave of fatigue, but he couldn't focus on it. He desired another weapon and desperately grabbed one of Amazarak's glowing boxes, ripped it from the table, and smashed it on Meeble's rising backside. Still hunkered over, Meeble turned about to receive another shimmering box on the head. Sparks and glass flew from the strange boxes. Rogan started to punch Meeble in the face, over and over, then he stared at the spearhead, the blood bubbling from the shoulder. He read the pain in the manner in which the creature moved and breathed.

While he appeared tired and certainly hurt, Meeble threw a quick elbow jab to Rogan's crotch, doubling him over. Rogan tried to put distance between them as the pain sank into his body from the groin strike. On all fours, Rogan's head turned up to see Meeble staggering, struggling to rise. He then wondered if this thing he fought truly was Meeble, or just a pretender. Rogan figured it didn't matter much as he'd be really dead if this Meeble crushed his skull. And...so would many more, not just this community in this realm, but his friends to the south, and in time, Albion.

Rogan stood again, legs shaking, pondering the worshipers of Meeble, and their campaigns of terror. "What a prick you are," Rogan muttered, thinking of the power and ability this thing possessed, and spent it on murder. Were the tales correct on the Thirteen? Were they from another universe and did Meeble do his bad things just to be an asshole to the Creator God? Why did the Creator God let this fuck do such things? Why wouldn't he stop him or slow him down?

In his head, Rogan heard laughter...not evil tones, but those of the Doorkeeper. Suddenly, it dawned on Rogan that while this unknown God didn't give him any special gift or power, he may have placed him in the right place to get in Meeble's way.

"A pawn again, in the game of the gods," Rogan laughed, angrier than before.

"Gods?" Meeble grumbled, also trying to get up and set his feet. "God kill my people. God must die."

With that statement, Meeble charged him and Rogan slipped away, sliding into the next line of tubes, pushing away two of the containers and letting them bounce and roll. Neither broke. Rogan hopped down, putting a tube between them, as Meeble pursued. He rolled it at the monster, who hopped over it with a crudely graceful gait, but the second tube he didn't navigate so well. Rogan had hoped he'd break it and more glass would be available to stab him with. The momentum of the tube went too far and Meeble got over it, almost. His left foot caught and Meeble stumbled, tripping over the tube, going flat to the floor.

As Meeble rolled over, Rogan navigated about him and rolled one of the tubes onto his midsection. Meeble floundered for a moment, grabbing the cylinder and trying to cast it away. Rogan countered, levering the container so Meeble hugged the top end to get a grip to throw it. Rogan leapt in the air, both boots together, and dropped on the end near Meeble's chest. From his weight and Meeble's grip, the glass broke and the container started to empty. Rogan landed, skidded in the fluid, but put his head and shoulders under the tube. He shoved it up so Meeble got the full bath in the face from the fluid. He heard Meeble gag and cough. Rogan let go of the tube and ran about the chest of Meeble as he cast off the annoying container. Rogan straddled his chest as the person in the tube flopped onto Meeble's legs. Rogan looked into Meeble's face, seeing his mouth open wide, full of the fluid, and his flat tongue poke out. He couldn't breathe.

"Drown, you cocksucker," Rogan roared and clasped his hands over Meeble's nose, trying to shut off any way he could breathe.

Meeble convulsed and his body went limp.

Rogan climbed off, sucking air himself, looking at Amazarak, who sported wide eyes.

"And you, ya sonofabitch, you brought him here," Rogan said in-between breaths, praying he had the strength to kill that fuck, too.

"Meeble broke your sword of steel, iron man of the mountains," Amazarak taunted him. "He broke a sword made by your father, I bet."

Meeble's body trembled and he coughed, fluid shooting from his nostrils.

Amazarak giggled, "He'll break you."

"My father didn't make that sword," Rogan muttered,

looking at the body from the tube that lazily lay across Meeble's legs. "Somebody else's dad made it."

Meeble vomited, not only the amber fluid down his gullet, but a black substance Rogan had only seen squirting from a child's ass immediately after birth.

Eyes on the person from the container, Rogan noted this individual wore a green outfit, almost a uniform, and carried a black weapon, that held a handgrip like a crossbow, but a long tube on it supported by bits of wood. Rogan picked this weapon up by the strap slung on it, and studied it. Rogan gripped the handle that sported a trigger like crossbows made in Shynar, but he saw no arrows to load in the barrel. He squeezed the trigger and nothing happened.

When Meeble started to sit up, Rogan gripped the weapon with his other hand and felt a latch give near the handle. Still gripping the device, he felt it explode in his grip…no…the explosions popped out the end of it, and sprayed into Meeble's injured shoulder, causing the creature to howl more. Rogan dropped the weapon, then picked it up. He pulled and squeezed and couldn't make it do that again. Cursing, he grabbed the weapon by the butt and drove it down like a spear into the wound beside the spearhead. Meeble howled, swinging over himself with his left hand, clouting Rogan's head and dropping him to his behind.

Meeble rose up, knees down, hands flat to support this rising, and flinched, the right shoulder still carrying the spearhead. He walked on his knees to get closer to Rogan and drew his left hand back to strike.

From his back, Rogan kicked both feet into the spearhead, shoving it further into Meeble's shoulder, and again, glancing off a bone in there. The left hand blow fell, but Meeble contorted, missing Rogan and striking the floor. To his knees, Rogan grabbed the end of the spearhead and twisted it, ripping to the side, grinding away from the bone joint inside Meeble and cleaving his flesh open further.

Meeble howled, got up, and staggered near to the second tube Rogan had let go that wasn't broken. For a moment, Meeble paused, waving his left hand in a circle. The tiny glowing disk started to expand in the air. Meeble then focused on Rogan and swung again. Rogan crouched, ducking the blow. He jumped up, grabbed the spearhead and hung by it, then dropping down, got ahold of Meeble's dangling arm and pulled it about behind his back. Rogan leapt as Meeble spun, trying to get a bead on his opponent. Rogan had swung about as Meeble turned, momentum carrying him around to curl his legs on Meeble's left arm from behind, all the while he chicken winged the brutal right arm under his body. Meeble screamed in pain as Rogan felt the shoulder pop out of the joint and the flesh shred further.

Rogan slid off Meeble's back, took a knee, and gave him another forearm to the balls. Meeble hunched again, and Rogan moved about him. Typically, Rogan could get any opponent up on his shoulders and break said enemy's back, but that move wouldn't be possible with Meeble. Rogan did the move in reverse, letting Meeble's hunched body drape over his shoulders. He pushed away with all his strength, separating Meeble from the earth and fell backwards, dropping the beast into the glass tube that had come to rest near the remains of the other. Meeble's body smashed through the glass and his howls deafened Rogan.

Rogan crawled off the debris and slid a few feet in the escaping amber water. Searching for his sword pieces, and spotting the soul jar of his grandson still sitting on the shelf not far from Amazarak, Rogan's knee hit the armored gloves of the shaman's suit of armor. He stood, picking up the right gauntlet, seeing the series of pointed fingertip knives. Rogan laughed, seeing Meeble struggling to rise in the mess, blood all over the side of him that impacted on the tube. Rogan put his hand in the metal glove, hardly fitting it in, but able to make the fingers work.

"Bastard," Meeble mouthed, gagging and trying to rise, but falling to his back in the debris.

Rogan stalked to him, metal glove extended out. He beat his chest with his left hand and shouted, "King!" He raised the right hand and stabbed down, pointing the fingertips at the gaping wound in Meeble's shoulder. The glove tore in deep. The cries rang loud and Meeble tried to rise, but Rogan dropped the gauntlet again and again. Then he stepped back, taking a slight slap to the face, but the blood from his nose only made the grin Rogan wore all the more cruel. Rogan shook off the gauntlet and grabbed Meeble's ruined right arm, twisted it about and fell back. With some effort, the arm separated completely, and Meeble's mouth opened so wide...and no sound came free.

Meeble flopped over, body convulsing, but up on his knees.

Rogan swung the arm like a bludgeon, striking Meeble's face with his own arm stump. Blood smeared his face and Meeble struggled to gasp. When Rogan reared back to strike again, Meeble's left hand shot out, grabbing at Rogan's throat, but seizing his jaw.

"Kill you," Meeble groaned, weak in his words. "Die, bastard king."

Rogan kicked back and freed himself from Meeble's grip. Again, he struggled with the arm of the creature that had come off, and it flipped about, the hand of Meeble in the face of its owner.

Meeble grabbed Rogan with his feet, getting on top, gripping the barbarian's thighs, left hand trying to strangle him. The dissected arm between them, Rogan and Meeble were near nose to nose. The arm between them was about all that saved Rogan as the weight of the monster bore down on him. Annoyed by the limb, Meeble tried to remove it with his chin, his body failing. Nowhere near as strong as before, Rogan thought.

Rogan forced his hands up between them, took the right hand of Meeble, and gripped the dew nail on the wrist. Meeble glared at him as Rogan forced the dew nail near to his left eye. Meeble dodged it, drawing his head to one side, but the dew nail caught on the edge of his eye socket. Rogan head-butted the hand and pulled, ripping the edge of Meeble's eye socket open, tearing flesh away, causing the eyeball to bulge out. Rogan embraced Meeble like a lover, but he didn't kiss him, he sank his teeth into the monster's eyeball, yanking the orb free.

Convulsing in new pain, Meeble pulled away, howling again, and putting his hand to his eye socket. Meeble tried to get up but his body had lost so much blood, he fell to his knees.

Rogan spat the eye of Meeble at Amazarak in the glass booth and missed. He then threw the arm of Meeble like a disk, impacting it on the glass booth Amazarak hid inside. The clear surface cracked and broke, and the shaman tumbled out onto the floor. Rogan breathed heavy, walking like a newborn colt over to the soul jar of his grandson, and spotting the broken sword he'd carried for so long. He gripped the pommel in his right hand and the jar in the other. They felt good in his hands.

"God damn..." Meeble hoarsely gasped, flat on his back, coughing more. "God...damn...you..."

Rogan roared, "God? Speak to me not of gods. It wasn't a god that laid you low, you sonofabitch, it was just a man." Rogan stood over him, straddling Meeble's head. "Take that into your void, disappear back into your labyrinth where all monsters hide. Carry into your dreams and waking moments that a simple savage sent you back into the dark, howling night!" Rogan slammed the soul jar into the empty cavity that once held Meeble's left eye. He then raised the broken sword and screamed, "WODAN!" The pommel dropped and his knees slammed on either side of Meeble's head. The handle of the sword smashed into the soul jar, driving it deep into Meeble's skull. Rogan gripped the edges of the pommel and forced it further into Meeble's head. Rogan didn't know if the soul jar entered what passed for Meeble's brain, but that move made the breath stop from the creature's lungs and the legs to stop kicking.

Amazarak slid against the wall, watching Rogan as the weary man stood, dropping the sword piece on Meeble's chest. He faced one of the glowing boxes still functioning and screamed.

Rogan's head raised and he stared at him. Out of breath, Rogan wondered, "Now, you scream like a bitch?"

"The power of my ship is compromised! The engines are critical!"

Rogan peered at the floating circle behind him, and thought it looked like a tunnel, one Meeble traveled through, one the shaman helped open.

"We are going to die!" Amazarak screamed, then turned, not expecting Rogan to be right in front of him.

"No, just you," Rogan grinned weakly, but his hands were apt enough to seize Amazarak by the arms and pull him near the portal, then swung him about.

The shaman skidded but stopped a foot away from the glowing disk. Eyes wide, he stared into it.

"The gate to the labyrinth!"

He turned to see Rogan running and executing a drop kick right into his chest. Amazarak flew backwards, his body folding into the portal swirls. Rogan hit the ground and watched the portal spin, shrink a little in size, but stay floating.

All around him the mountain shook and the metal trim started to fall from the walls. Rogan peered into the gateway and saw things, faces he couldn't recognize and a horror that should never be named. He ran from the room and the machines about him howled.

Rogan ran as the mountain shook around him. He ran for the light of the outside, but was soon blinded. He fell into light and then darkness.

11 DEPARTURES

ROGAN'S EYES OPENED to see Javan staring at him, looking relieved. He then scanned the area, seeing only the red braves he brought up the hill, exhausted, spent, but grinning. Rogan also saw a weak looking Akibeel, free from the sabers.

The cave and mountain top were a pile of rubble. Trees were sticking out at bizarre angles as if a child were dissatisfied with their toy construction and destroyed it.

"Sire!" Javan said. "It was spectacular! The mountain came down. It destroyed itself and Amazarak died just outside here, his heart burst through his chest."

Rogan nodded and sat up, seeing Asenka laying on the ground, her chest not moving and blood all over her. Zenata knelt, weeping by her side.

"I saw some of it." He looked away from her body. "I saw what destiny has in store for those who dare defy the simple edicts of Wodan."

Javan, confused, asked, "What are you saying?"

"My grandson, unborn, his soul was caught in transit, was given blessing by Wodan to live and fight, but that bastard wizard across the sea set him loose and that shaman Amazarak imprisoned him. Loosed and invoked, I think Wodan took back his gift. At least, that is all that makes sense of that nightmare in there. He was disturbed from his boredom with humanity. Wodan looked out the corner of his eye and saw me. Rhiannon help me, with eyes like glacial ice, he saw me and was angry, but he turned and saw those who mocked him…pretended to be him…and stole his gift."

"But what happened to the mountain? What happened to Amazarak?"

"Wodan shrugged." He coughed and lay back again. "Amazarak was cast into a hole ripped in the air, fell into eternity. But I faced a member of the Thirteen, Javan."

Javan gave him a questioning look. "Really, sire?"

Forearm over his eyes, Rogan replied, "I'm not crazy. I battled Meeble himself."

"And how did that go?"

"I won. He's in pieces in there under the mountain, inasmuch as anything like him can die. I think I sent his form away from here, but who knows if he can manifest again, given enough flesh and souls?"

"Asenka…" Javan said, but stopped speaking.

Rogan didn't look over again. "I see. Perhaps she's the luckiest one on this mountain."

With workman-like purpose and with not many words involved, the tribesmen tore down the poles of the red lodge of Amazarak. While they performed this task, uttering curses on the pieces, like they themselves contained evil, they took note of Rogan and Javan, working elsewhere in the clearing.

Gathering up a mound of branches, they created a thick bed to which Rogan carried the body of Asenka. Rogan put her on the mound with great care, like he handled a child that still breathed. He stood back and none drew near him, not even Javan, until he turned to face them. Rogan picked up her bow and placed the weapon across her body, chin to pelvis. His blue eyes looked at her as his tired face remained expressionless.

Javan broke the silence. "Sire?"

Rogan looked to the sky and then turned away from him. He said to Zenata, "Say a prayer to her gods, girl. We must go down the mountain."

Looking slightly hurt, Javan patted her back and pushed her forward to say her prayers. The girl still stood stunned and Javan whispered, "He is as he is. Please do as he asks."

"Bastard," she muttered as she began to pray.

Wearing the word like a crown, Rogan walked from them and stared into the sky. For a moment Rogan thought he saw an object, like a gigantic bird far off. He blinked and it was gone.

The braves grew near to the mound, struck flints, and in time, Asenka was afire. The embers rose up and flew off into the air.

"Her gods will carry her spirit home," Rogan said quietly. "I have a meeting with my gods coming soon. The road of the gods will be well traveled before that day, however."

Tears exploding from her eyes, hands clenched to fists, Zenata raged at Rogan, "Is that all you can say for her?"

Rogan looked at the body afire and then to the girl. "She made me happy for a little while. I'm sure she felt the same, but please don't make my ass heavy with romantic thoughts. Save them for my nephew, who still has heart enough to give more than a fuck about tomorrow."

"But..." she choked.

He raged, "There is no tomorrow!"

"Enough," Javan yelled back as Zenata buried her face in his chest. He gave Rogan a stern look, one of distaste, and the old one yanked his gaze from that of his nephew.

"Let's go. I'm so tired I could die."

Still holding the girl, Javan wondered, "Then why don't you?"

"Patience, Javan." Rogan's eyes again set on him, but this time the weary sarcasm had vanished, replaced by a wolfish bloodlust. "I've got a few more things to do yet before I leave."

Rogan and his band of rough savages came down the mountain, looking back up to the misty wreath capped flat. So much information flooded his mind, but Rogan dealt with it as always. Even when they stopped to sleep, Rogan's primal fury for the enemies far off boiled paramount in his self. All mysteries or evils were naught compared with the desire to survive. Yes, he'd take the look, smell, and taste of Meeble to eternity, but that had passed. No longer did he seek after a glorious demise. That notion vanished in his aging mind to be replaced by the bloodthirsty revenge for those destroying Albion. Though he told himself that land would've been better with his son in charge, no man should slay his kindred and live. Rogan would return and die in a realm near to where he was born, he reasoned. Then, he'd rest. However, he didn't care if he kept the survivors up with his snoring.

In the night, his mind ran full of plans to sail south in the injured ship and return to Olmek-Tikal. Rogan figured that with these men in tow he could persuade his friends in Olmek-Tikal to return to the lands from hence he came. They wouldn't dare deny him this, he wagered, and Rogan knew he had to get back. If any of the visions were true, he must return home.

The next morning, Javan exclaimed, "Sire, look!" He pointed amongst the trees toward the sky.

Though shrouded in branches, Rogan could perceive a circled creature with long leathery wings. It flew lower than usual and Rogan sighed in disgust. "Wish that we could shoot that bastard thing down." He grabbed his groin. "Yeah, you prick, I'm comin' for you all."

Akibeel favored his walking stick a great deal and shook his head from side to side. "No, Rogan. I feel this time it is different."

"What say you?" Rogan asked, taking his eyes from the sky.

"That thing is not here for seeing of sights," the shaman said and gestured up. "Look!"

The winged creature grew larger in their eyes and came at them fast.

Gritting his teeth, Rogan drew his short sword and Javan slotted in two arrows in the heavy bow. The company of men traveling down the raw trail that morning were frozen as the creature extended his wings and revealed the true horror of its appearance. Slender and lithe, yet covered in raised spikes like a crocodile, the short mouth of the semi-human winged beast opened and roared. Javan released his arrows, yet only one pierced the beast's left wing. The monster came right at Rogan, who dropped to the grass, anticipating the creature's flight path. Rogan ducked low enough, but the claws of the creature's feet gripped his shoulders. Before the nails could sink in, Rogan's timing proved perfect...for he stabbed up between the flailing legs. Near to a foot of Rogan's short sword entered the creature's crotch and it howled...but not as much as when Rogan forced his sword forward, not sliding it back the way it came. The beast kept aloft, yet Rogan ripped loose the beast's bowels.

Akibeel shouted to his red warriors, breaking their astonishment. Soon, these men fixed arrows and fired.

Dozens of arrows filled the beast and it faltered in the sky. Rogan drew back his short sword and roared, throwing it end over end. The blade impaled the monster in the chest and pinned it to a tree trunk. Javan and Rogan each grabbed a clawed foot and yanked, tearing the creature off the sword and practically ripping it in half.

"Wodan, what sort of beast is this?" Javan asked.

Akibeel declared, "A creation of high wizardry. This beast is part human and part homunculus. It is fed by bile from afar."

Rogan retrieved his sword and spat on the face of the dead beast. "I saw it in the vision, a child of the wizard woman in Albion. If that bitch wants a piece of me, then let her bastards come for me in droves if they must. I'm coming for her now."

At the beach when he saw the giant ocean fairing ship in the distance and the small landing boats at the sand, Rogan's heart surged. *These were men from Olmek-Tikal obviously searching for his fishing party days overdue!* Javan was far ahead of him, shouting for them. These tribal men were distant cousins to these red skinned savages. Their skin tone a bronze color and their hair an even brown, not completely black in places. A far more educated folk, these peoples practically worshiped Rogan and his friends from afar. Even if he made them stop their human sacrifices, they were intelligent enough to see the modern way of a barbarian life.

The other strange thing was the bireme was righted in the water. At first, Rogan thought this the work of the Olmek-Tikal folk, but soon saw that the women of the Kennebeck tribe had done this act.

Rogan looked at Akibeel and the shaman grinned. "I knew we would win and return, so I ordered them to repair your ship."

With a huge hand, Rogan motioned to the large galley vessel in the ocean and said, "It may be unnecessary. Wodan!"

Rogan made no fast run to these people from Olmek-Tikal. He let Javan relay what happened to those from the south. Rogan recognized the Olmek-Tikal leader, Xuxan, nodding to Javan's words. The slender Olmek-Tikalize fighter grinned at the sight of Rogan and gestured at the large galley beyond.

He said to Rogan, "So, Rogan, I see war follows you wherever you travel."

Rogan snorted. "Aye, damn them all. I'm actually glad to see your skinny ass, Xuxan."

"Javan tells me of the hazard in your homeland," Xuxan said calmly, then directed his eyes up at the misty mountain. "He tells me of the perils had here, as well."

"Javan can talk too much. Do you have any wine?"

Xuxan laughed. "We have a great crew and some supplies on the ship, but not an army to aide you, if you truly seek to return at this time."

"I do seek to do so," Rogan said roughly, staring across the ocean as if he could see the threat waiting him there. He glanced at the savages behind him and said, "Fear not,

Xuxan. I have a force of fighters willing to fight for me here if your sailors haven't the balls for the trip."

Xuxan gave the Kennebeck a doubtful look but shrugged. "I see. You will return with these?"

"Yes, blast you. Now isn't the time to argue who is smarter amongst you all. They will fight and have faced a great demon today. Getting them to my homeland will be vile work on the sea, perhaps. I know not what has happened in Albion for certain. It's all words from wizards and dreams in the mind."

Xuxan sighed, well aware of the old man's thoughts on wizards. "Since there is no talking to you, bull-headed man, I shall see you there too."

"Saves me the time of taking your ship, then, by Wodan!"

Xuxan smiled and gave Rogan a mock slap on the shoulder. "We best go now and not wait. The journey will take some time."

Rogan nodded, again staring at the waves, then at the ship akin to a fine woman. "I fear time is not on our side, my friend."

The craft was a good sized three-masted vessel with a distinctive hull sporting a pronounced overhanging bow and stern. Rogan thought that a corsair would kill for the speed and space of this vessel. They were built with a narrow floor to achieve a higher speed than their victims, but with a considerable beam in order to enable them to carry an extensive sail plan. This one could hold a crew of 300 to 400 men. A lugsail rig was added to the design as well, when a mizzen was stepped right aft. This provided a better balance of sail power and avoided to a great extent the disability of the lateen sail, the immense length of the yard on which the sail was set and the need when tacking and to lower the sail in order to bring the yard to the other side of the mast.

With this, Rogan knew, they would get home fast.

He faced Javan and then Zenata, who held his nephew's hand. "Coming along, girl?"

"Yes." She looked at Javan. "He is all I have now."

Rogan smirked, but walked past them both. "Me, too."

When he walked up to the water, he heard Zenata say to Javan, "What does Rogan really mean?"

"What?"

"Power does come in naming, Javan, and we name our children well. I wonder after his meaning."

"Rogan can mean different things, but I've always heard it postulated that it means what is most fitting."

"And that is?'

"King of the bastards."

CODA
EPILOGUE TO A YARN

THE STORYTELLER FINISHED his yarn and leaned back on the ship to rest.

Looking out at the blue, almost translucent waves, Magog then gawked at his brother Gomer before saying, "Father, are you saying King Rogan the Great was our grandfather?"

"Yes, boys. He was a mighty warrior that went on to even more adventure."

Gomer spoke up and said, "Then Mother, Algeniz, she really was almost sacrificed?"

"Yes, boys."

Gomer asked with glee, "Tell us more! Did Grandfather encounter more of the Thirteen? He and Javan must've returned to Albion!"

Magog elbowed his brother aside. "I heard the story that he visited the Land of Nodd!"

"That's a tale for another day, my boys, as is the one of how they returned to Albion and what they found there. We must help my father tend the animals."

A female voice called from below the massive deck. "Come along, all of you, and stop telling such yarns, Jasper Thal!"

Magog blinked. "What did Mother say?"

"Never mind."

"But, Father," Magog persisted. "Your name isn't Jasper Thal!"

"Ah yes, but that's how they said my name when I took the tale concerning the end of the world to the corners of the Earth. No one listened and that's why only we are spared the great cataclysm. Jasper Thal is the way the Albions said my name, Japheth."

"And those of the demonic horde laughed at the words of the Wiseman in the seventh heaven. And yet, he spoke to us with great scorn. Woe to those who build up kingdoms of iniquity and oppression; and who lay their foundations in fraud. For suddenly, they will be subverted, never to obtain peace. Woe to you who build up houses on crime; for they will have foundations that break and by their swords they themselves shall fall. You have committed great blasphemy and iniquity and are destined to the day of effusion of blood, unto the day of darkness, and to the day of great judgment. This I declare and point out to you, that he who created you will destroy you."

From Fragment XXVI of the Third Yee-wa

ABOUT THE AUTHORS

BRIAN KEENE writes novels, comic books, short fiction, and occasional journalism for money. He is the author of over forty books, mostly in the horror, crime, and dark fantasy genres. Keene's novels have been translated into German, Spanish, Polish, Italian, French, Taiwanese, and many more. In addition to his own original work, Keene has written for media properties such as *Doctor Who*, *Hellboy*, *Masters of the Universe*, and *The X-Files*.

Several of Keene's novels have been developed for film, including *Ghoul*, *The Ties That Bind*, and *Fast Zombies Suck*. Several more are in-development or under option. Keene also serves as Executive Producer for the independent film studio Drunken Tentacle Productions. Keene also oversees Maelstrom, his own small press publishing imprint specializing in collectible limited editions, via Thunderstorm Books.

Keene's work has been praised in such diverse places as *The New York Times*, *The History Channel*, *The Howard Stern Show*, *CNN.com*, *Publisher's Weekly*, *Media Bistro*, *Fangoria Magazine*, and *Rue Morgue Magazine*. He has won numerous awards and honors, including the World Horror Grandmaster Award, and a recognition from Whiteman A.F.B. (home of the B-2 Stealth Bomber) for his outreach to U.S. troops serving both overseas and abroad. A prolific public speaker, Keene has delivered talks at conventions, college campuses, theaters, and inside Central Intelligence Agency headquarters in Langley, VA.

The father of two sons, Keene lives in rural Pennsylvania.

STEVEN L. SHREWSBURY lives, works and writes one day at a time. Over 365 of his short stories have been published in print or digital media since the late 80s along with over 100 of his poems. He writes in the realms of horror and sword & sorcery. His novels include *Within, Philistine, Overkill, Hell Billy, Blood & Steel, Thrall, Stronger Than Death, Hawg, Thoroughbred, Tormentor, Godforsaken* and the just released *Born of Swords*.

He has collaborated with other writers, like Peter Welmerink in *Bedlam Unleashed*, Nate Southard in *Bad Magick*, and Maurice Broaddus in the forthcoming *Black Son Rising*.

After 26 years working in printing, Shrewsbury now works in the field of AgriScience.

He is the father of two sons. Shrewsbury lives in rural Central Illinois. He continues to search for brightness in this world, no matter where it chooses to hide.

ABOUT THE ARTIST

DANIEL KAMARUDIN is a freelance Concept Artist/ Illustrator based in Brunei who specializes in fantasy art and character design. He started delving into art in high school where he designed armors and environments inspired by video games like *World of Warcraft* and *Dragon Age*.

His works can be seen on various novel covers such as *The Starfall Knight, Forging Divinity*, and the *Whill of Agora* series.

You can view more of Daniel's works at:

theDURRRRIAN.Deviantart.com

or

theDURRRRIAN.tumblr.com .

APEX PUBLICATIONS NEWSLETTER

Why sign up?

Newsletter-only promotions. Book release announcements. Event invitations. And much, much more!

SUBSCRIBE AND RECEIVE A **15%** DISCOUNT CODE FOR YOUR NEXT ORDER FROM APEXBOOKCOMPANY.COM!

If you choose to sign up for the Apex Publications newsletter, we will send you an email confirmation to insure that you in fact requested the newsletter and to avoid unwanted emails. Your email address is always kept confidential, and we will only use it to send you newsletters or special announcements. You may unsubscribe at any time, and details on how to unsubscribe are included in every newsletter email.

VISIT
HTTP://WWW.APEXBOOKCOMPANY.COM/PAGES/NEWSLETTER

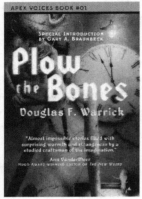

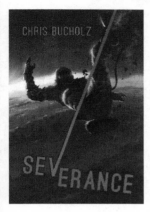

THE LOST LEVEL

Apex is proud to present the first book in Grand Master Award winner Brian Keene's long-awaited new series, a loving ode to lost world classics like Burroughs's PELLUCIDAR, Howard's ALMURIC, and Lansdale's THE DRIVE-IN, but with a thoroughly modern twist that only Brian Keene could conceive.

BY BRIAN KEENE

"Brian Keene's new novel, *The Lost Level*, goes a long way towards capturing that feeling of headlong adventure on another world."
Singular Points, Charles R. Rutledge

"...there's simply no way I can't recommend it—it's probably the most well-written "pulp" novel you'll ever read, and its characters will stick with you the same way your favorite comic characters did as a kid. Keene has always specialized in relatable characters, and the same is true here."
Horrordrive-in.com, Frank Pharaoh

ISBN: 978-1-937009-10-6   ~   ApexBookCompany.com

Made in the USA
Columbia, SC
29 September 2017